"Folk has come a long way since the 'folk boom' of the 1960s (or 'great folk scare' as some refer to it), and despite predictions to the contrary, folk is more vibrant and popular than ever. Andy Beck spins a tale that shows us how folk musicians can earn a living doing what they love."

- Dan Murphy, 'The Acoustic Outpost'

"A rewarding read. Well written, engaging and insightful. A voyage into the lives and minds of struggling musicians, and a glimpse into the battles that every man and woman with a dream must face."

- Joe Barnes, author of *Do The Work You Love*

"Anyone who has ever stepped on stage as a musician, or watched from the audience, will love this book. People making music, and music making people; a wonderful, rip-roaring ride through life at its dreamy, devoted, detuned and drunken best!"

- Michael Klevenhaus, founder of the German Centre for Gaelic Language and Culture

FOLK
SPRINGS
ETERNAL

FOUR MUSICIANS
HAD A DREAM.
THEIR SUCCESS WILL HELP
YOU FIND YOURS.

ANDY BECK

ANDY BECK
PRODUCTIONS

Printed in the United States of America

Published by Andy Beck Productions
Unit 38936, PO Box 6945, London, W1A 6US,
United Kingdom
http://www.andybeckwriting.com/

Identifiers:
ISBN: 978-1-5272-6468-7 (paperback)
ISBN: 978-1-5272-6469-4 (hardback)
ISBN: 978-1-5272-6470-0 (e-book)

Available in paperback, hardback, and e-book formats.
Audiobook due subsequently.

Illustrations by Ina Dziggel.
Illustration #5 adapted from *Matterhorn*
by Nicole Regina Hunziker.
Used with kind permission.

Cover design by Jetlaunch.

AT THAT MOMENT, LIN KNEW EXACTLY
WHAT THEY NEEDED TO DO.
NEW TEARS BEGAN TO BREAK IN HER EYES.
THEY WERE TEARS OF RELIEF.
TEARS OF *JOY*.

Table of Contents

Free Song. xi

Part One: Passion

Chapter One – Folk-Punk 3

Chapter Two – Remember the Tune 13

Part Two: Stumbling Blocks

Chapter Three – Pessimism 21

Chapter Four – The Rules of Society. 35

Part Three: Trial by Fire

Chapter Five – Degrading and Frightening 49

Chapter Six – Why We Don't Walk Alone 67

Chapter Seven – Horror 75

Chapter Eight – They Don't Want Us 97

Part Four: The Outcome

Chapter Nine – The Pain. 109

Chapter Ten – The Reward 129

Action Plan

How to Follow Your Own Dreams 135

Acknowledgments

I would like to thank the following people:

- My family and friends, especially those who share my passion for folk music and Celtic culture;

- All the "ignited souls" in my life —your motivation and guidance have made this book possible;

- Stan Rogers, a Canadian legend, whose song "Barrett's Privateers" motivated me to strive for similar accuracy of detail;

- Kerstin, my wife. For your undying love, patience and support.

Free Song

To give you an idea of the music genre around which this story is based, I have written and recorded a short piece of folk music for you to enjoy on all the major streaming platforms. The piece is an instrumental, entitled "Cate Maguire's Polka", and listed under my artist name of CALE.

To find the song quickly, you can scan the Spotify code below:

If you have difficulty accessing the song, or are not familiar with streaming, you can reach me by email on info@andybeckwriting.com. I will then send you the track.

With thanks to Markus Pede, who played the bodhrán (Irish frame drum) for the piece!

PART ONE
Passion

CAIBIDEIL A H-AON
CHAPTER ONE

Folk-Punk

Feb 20ᵗʰ, The Bottle of Smoke

Rash didn't need a count-in, nor any accompaniment from Lin. Buzzing with the emotional charge of the evening, the accordion player stomped his foot on the pub's oak floorboards and went straight into the opening riff of "The Orcadian". After four bars, Lin cracked her tipper against the skin of her *bodhrán*, the Irish frame drum, and the band was in full swing. Following them beat-for-beat were the three *cèilidh* dancers, one of whom had not yet introduced himself. Others attempted to learn the steps as Guthrie (Gus, for short) led the sonic onslaught with his trademark, Lagavulin-lubricated growl. The occasional curse word from the singer bothered no-one, at least not when the music made you feel like this.

And life on the edge was dismal and dredge
The penny too black to glisten
You took all the more to feel insecure
You never stop to listen
As the Downies clawed themselves out of their dens
Went up to Gills and then over the end
They'll fuck, they'll fight, they'll scratch and they'll bite
While up in the air you're wasting your life

Where Gus pulled lines like these from was anyone's guess. A prolific and gifted lyricist, he'd admitted that alcohol was sometimes of assistance, as if his bandmates hadn't already known. But they were still very different from the lyrics he'd written when the group had been called Skylight. Better suited to folk music on the whole, but also more obscure, a gutter-hymn form of poetry. It didn't matter. The audience loved it, the rest of the band loved it, other bands they'd played with liked it—hell, even some of the venue owners and managers had admitted to liking it. What Gus did give away was how much The Pogues inspired him, and the parallels between his work and the raucous drinking songs of the London Irish legends were sometimes patent. Though he didn't quite share the thin, shabby look of Shane MacGowan, nor even his penchant for self-destruction, it was undeniable that Gus was a musical and lyrical genius, one who could weave magic from the very ordinary.

It was the third time already this year that the band had played their favourite pub. On this particular occasion, the honour had initially been a mysterious one. "Just come down and we'll get ya set up," was all Management had said on the phone. As it turned out, they'd neglected to plan anything special for the evening and, keen on a boost in profits, they'd turned to the band for help. Wednesday night or no Wednesday night, it was paying off; over fifty people in, takings at the bar into quadruple figures, and little sign of the evening slowing down, work tomorrow be damned. If this was any indication of how St. Patrick's Day would go, then *sick*, as the colloquialism went.

The quartet reached the song's instrumental mid-section. Rash's accordion kept apace with the metallic sweep-picking of Herman's mandolin, while Gus punctuated the electric atmosphere with a yell or two. The buoyant, alcohol-fuelled dancing continued as the bartenders brought fresh Guinness, Murphy's and Belhaven to the surrounding tables, where guests both young and old sat clapping along, having a great time and (for the most part) neglecting to look at their phones. On a Friday or Saturday night the first sparks of a cigarette lighter would have gone up by now, as past a certain point most people simply stopped caring about the smoking ban. Fitting, then, that THE BOTTLE OF SMOKE was the name adorning the sign above Halifax's oldest Irish pub.

Graduating to folk music was certainly the smartest move the band had ever made. Attendance at gigs and overall enthusiasm around their music had increased notably since the days of Skylight. Back then, tangible successes had been few and far between—too few and too far for a group of musicians talking about *making it, taking things forward, living the dream* and so forth. The group had ultimately put the lacklustre gigs and poor pay down to their chosen genre of *post-hardcore* music, the sheer volume and distortion of which had been enough to keep many potential attendees away. While some of their musical heroes (such as the Ontario-born Alexisonfire) had achieved substantial success in this field, to Herman's mind it was counterproductive when the soundmen at local gigs cranked the PA so loud you could barely hear the music, let alone yourself think. All too often, the sound would blur to a screechy, reverberating drone interspersed with the drummer thrashing the hell out of the kit. Up-and-coming local bands stood little chance like that, no matter how good their music, and when you were just one of many the odds were even less favourable. It hadn't been for want of trying, either; as Skylight, they'd done everything from festivals and pay-to-play affairs, to supporting overseas acts at bigger venues and planning mini-tours as cost-effectively as possible. In the end, they'd gutted it all of its worth, with very little to show for their efforts.

The Skylight chapter had ended after one particularly depressing Saturday night, where half the people in the sparsely populated room had simply walked out halfway through the band's opening number. After the gig, which the band had left early in a huff, Gus and Tamila (being Lin's real name) had stayed up talking till three in the morning. The next day, they called a band meeting. "Cards-on-the-table time," the singer had begun. "I've had enough. I *don't* want to be in a band that's going nowhere, playing to no-one, and earning jack shit." He was also tired of screaming his lungs out on stage and going home half-deaf. Lin, while less profane, had been in agreement with her cousin. "We can do better. We certainly *deserve* better."

The pair weren't just asking for more; they were suggesting a change in musical direction, a shift to something quieter and more audience-friendly. They managed to persuade Herman, easily the most decisive and musically gifted of the other three. However, bassist Nina gave no conclusive response to anything and, without explicitly announcing her departure, quietly shuffled out of the café (and with it, the band). Rhythm guitarist Mitch was more reactive, arguing the case for retaining a heavy rock sound, but this only led to a heated disagreement between him and Gus. Twenty minutes later and Mitch was gone too, without having said goodbye. "I don't care," Gus would say later. "It needed to be said. I'm sick of us lying to ourselves."

Stripped back to a trio, the band debated as to which "quieter" genre to turn to. After a period of indecision, they opted for a less-distorted, more laid-back sound, with Herman's electric guitar left in the line-up but the explosive riffs and pounding drums gone. Changing their name to Twilight Sky, they recruited a new bassist in Michael, wrote ten strong enough songs, and recorded an EP that one online reviewer compared favourably to British indie rockers Athlete. They also played a dozen shows at venues they deemed "worth doing", some of which would, in fact, pay better. But it still wasn't enough. Gus admitted to struggling with writing music of a less abrasive nature, complaining that he "needed to go for the balls" more. Meanwhile, Michael left after just six months. And so the band was faced with a dilemma; write songs with a rough edge, but steer clear of the noise and the clutter. How to proceed?

Two weeks later, on a wet night in March, Gus knocked on a fever-ridden Lin's door at the sociable hour of 12.15am. He'd found the answer in an unlikely place. Having happened by The Bottle of Smoke earlier that evening (which, even with his knowledge of the neighbourhood's hangouts, he'd only ever been in twice), he'd decided on a pint or two, partly to get out of the rain but also to stave off the curse of Monday morning. At 8.30pm, a band in their late twenties called The Rebel O'Keefes, who Gus had never heard of, had walked on stage and proceeded to play. Their music stopped him cold. This wasn't inaudible, 100-decibel "music to cut your throat by", as Lin's stepdad Mark had once scorned the post-hardcore scene. Nor was it "music for grannies", as Gus himself had often dismissed the folk genre. This was something different; an infectious mix of Irish and Scottish rebel songs, catchy *tunes* (instrumentals), drinking songs and, yes, one or two well-known covers. It was above all the rebel songs, with their anti-imperialist sentiment, that made Gus sit up and listen. They were punky, they were potent, they were provocative. And yet it was acoustic music! Played on a steel-string guitar, mandolin and cajón, producing a blend that was both joyous and romantic. "And you could hear it for once!" Gus would enthuse to Lin that night, before falling asleep on her mum's couch. He'd stayed until the end, soaking up the atmosphere (and a few Guinnesses) and pleasantly surprised by the number of people sitting around watching, fifty or sixty over the course of the evening. The notion that acoustic music could unleash just as much power as walls of distorted guitar, if not more, was a peculiar and unexpected paradox. At the end, while the O'Keefes were packing up, one of the barmen walked up to their vocalist and stuffed a wad of cash into his hand. Five hundred dollars, in Gus's estimation. That had been the clincher. "I ain't a moneyhead," he swore to Lin and Herman the very next day, "but that's what musicians SHOULD get paid." Maybe it wasn't "music for grannies" after all.

With fresh hope, and a new course plotted in his mind, Gus now needed to convince his bandmates. Lin gave the O'Keefes and the slightly rockier Mahones (another gang of Ontario legends) a good listen, and decided she was on board. Willing to give folk music a chance, she got over her cold, ditched her drumsticks and bought a cheap cajón to bang on. Before long, she graduated to the bodhrán, and grew quickly in confidence and competence. Herman, meanwhile, was harder to talk round; initially in favour of giving Twilight Sky a longer run at it, he wasn't sure if he wanted to play Celtic music. Amid Gus's insistence that they would not be abandoning their semi-nihilistic punk influences, what ultimately convinced Herman was St. Patrick's Day, which as chance would have it was just nine days later. The three of them returned to The Smoke, which this time was packed to the brim, and again the O'Keefes were playing, sharing the stage with a more experienced group from Montréal called Shinrone, who primarily played *trad* (traditional pieces) but were no less enjoyable.

It was a beautiful, perfect evening. One of the finest the trio had shared in the time they'd known each other. Great music, heartfelt melodies, inspiring conversations with people from diverse backgrounds, drinking, dancing, smoking, the lot. And again, the money was above and beyond anything Gus, Lin and Herman were used to, with both bands walking out with a full $1,000. Herman admitted to being emotionally spent the next day; sad that the evening was over, but jubilant that something in his life had changed. "I can't believe we ignored this for so long," were his exact words.

The three of them became regulars at The Smoke after that. Soon, they opted to change the band name again, this time to something completely different. While Gus resumed [acoustic] guitar and vocal duties, and Lin continued to progress well with the frame drum, Herman picked up a mandolin that an acquaintance of his didn't want. Between then and now, they'd all become proficient, and Herman had taken it upon himself to learn the tin whistle too, swiftly becoming hooked as he now owned five of them. "One day, when we have the money," he would promise the others, "I'll learn to play the Scottish smallpipes."

The new music was certainly ideal for keeping this February's dismal weather from the door. It didn't matter how unpredictable the rain was, nor how many evenings the wind howled between the buildings and around the eaves. Tonight, with music in their ears, stout in their bellies and fire in their hearts, things were just dandy. And Rash's accordion was always a welcome addition at the bigger gigs. Their newest member, who'd started life as a pianist, played on all of the band's recordings, contributed songwriting ideas and took part in every decision they made. Only at the smaller venues did it make little sense to bring more than three musicians along, owing either to limited stage space or the lesser pay. One example was The Punch Bowl, a cosy little place along the 103 that booked the band once every few months and paid $300 (though as a family joint, it meant Gus had to rein in the foul language and boozing somewhat). Otherwise, adding the accordion had been every inch the sensible idea; the instrument paired beautifully with the mandolin, and Rash's left-hand parts injected enough low-end energy to replace the bass guitar, the band having been loath to add one after their previous experiences of the damned instrument rumbling, masking the other frequencies above it in a live setting. On their self-titled debut album, which had been finished and self-released just before Christmas, Herman had added some bass, and in the studio it had mixed well.

"The Orcadian" ended as abruptly as it had started, all four musicians part-singing and part-yelling the last four syllables. If that always felt good, it was better still when some of the audience knew the words and joined in. Applause and cheers went up around the room; Rash and Herman fist-bumped on a job well done, while Lin necked the top of her Belhaven and Gus checked his tuning for the next number. Three more songs, including one sung by Lin in the other language, and a second break would be in order. The band would then return for their final set, and probably an encore. Both could be used to promote the CD, to try and sell a copy or two. Whenever the musicians were not interacting with the audience during a break, they would spend their time taking the air, having a smoke or a vape (Gus, Lin and very occasionally Herman), and discussing anything ranging from music, alcohol, women and suggestive jokes to films, documentaries, animal rights, veganism, and the art of being *straight edge*. The last two of these were Rash's specialities. The more drink the other three consumed, the freer the conversation would flow, and once in a while it would slow right down when they split a spliff after the gig, at which point Rash would excuse himself until they were done. As the designated driver, no-one gave him a hard time over it. The four were united; joined by a solid friendship and a mutual love of folk-punk music. Music that offered so much life, so much energy. So much hope.

As for success, the sky was the limit.

CAIBIDEIL A DHÀ
CHAPTER TWO

Remember the Tune

Feb 26th, Parkland Drive, Clayton Park West

The day around is pleasant, a soft breeze caressing the long, green blades of grass. Josefine's wearing her black trousers and white blouse, that nut-brown hair of hers tied back and some of it falling behind her ears. To me, she's always been quite pretty. And she's started to play; her left hand graces the surface of her bodhrán (that expensive signature one from her videos) as her other hand slides up and down the skin. She sits on her short, black stool; sometimes it's one of The Smoke's wooden bar stools, quite tall. And then her gentle, honey-sweet voice chimes into view as butterflies flutter and she starts to sing the song she just made up.

Low, low the river flows along the valley-o
Dry on dry, as it fails up the mountainside
General MacArthur's come home to see his sons
And if the circle goes five times around
There'll be whisky on the ground

It's in the key of C. Josefine's from Munich, but there's no trace of a German accent in her voice. Not when she sings, anyway. And she never trips up—her playing is perfectly smooth, some difficult triples thrown in there but she never misses a beat. The first clusters of cloud gather over the rolling Holyrood ridges as she turns on the Scottish Gaelic (and the style).

'S ann bha 'n othail aig an fhadhail.

She sings it twice before she has to slow down and stop. Looking over, she asks me something: "What's that first part in English? Erm…'What a confusion'?" "*Nein*," comes the unhesitating call from Herman—he's standing off to the right, in the same clothes he wore on Heritage Day. This guy's never wrong when it comes to languages. "*Commotion*," he corrects her. "'What a commotion there was.'" I nod in agreement. Josefine does that look she sometimes does—it means she's thinking. Then she goes, "oh yeah", smirks and picks up where she left off, singing the line again. Her momentum builds and she starts to speed up, the lyrics becoming more rapid-fire.

The atmosphere takes on an eerie, uneasier air as the clouds thicken above. Jo's singing is just as serene, but it's faster, and so is her playing. It's almost tribal now as the pounding hooves (some of the horses are brown, some are white) come ripping along the battlefield. The first swords are drawn from their sheaths, they're long, pointy and melty, and here comes Tim from work, tracing the ground with his as he bounds past me several times and out of shot. And Barbara Hill (yes, it *is* her) is there too, a hand to her helmet as she barks a long order, calls for backup or maybe she's calling her husband on that stupidly expensive phone she bought. The atmosphere is frantic now—cries of war go up around the periphery. And still Josefine's technique is constant, her voice never falters as it starts to repeat and fade. *And if the circle comes five times around, there'll be whisky on the ground.* The day fades to black, but it didn't rain.

A little while later, it does start to rain. Falling softly at first, it soon pelts loudly on the barn's old but robust wooden roof. There are drips here and there, little leaks, but not here in the warm and golden middle where Maxine and I sit on the hay. Maxine's a physiotherapist in her 40s; but secretly, I know she likes it wild. She sips her Shiraz and asks me what my instrument's made of. "Erm, goatskin," I say to her, trying not to sound nervous. "Or it can be synthetic, non-animal. Sometimes they make it from cow." The shadows around us take half an interest as they drift in and out; one is the blonde woman who always orders a large mocha, another is that IT guy with brown hair and glasses from the M&M's commercial. I prop the bodhrán up on my thigh, and continue to advise. "You can tune it too. To D, or G. Or Z sharp. I've got loads of tippers." I pick the first one up, blow the hay away, and try to strike the drumskin. But I keep missing. It just *won't* go through, no matter what I try or what convoluted angle I come at the drum from.

I keep reaching back to it, but now Maxine's pulling me away. She's smiling at me, seductively, crawling over me on all feline fours. Her leathers crackle and her dyed black hair (slightly longer than mine) is thick as forest as I run my fingers through it. "Call me Max, sweetie," she says in an irresistible voice. I don't give a shit she's 46. I drink in her deep, brown eyes while her soft-hard palms and long, powerful limbs dominate me. I lie back, giving her complete control, and slowly I can feel it coming while all around us the cosy, cavernous barn shelters us from the storm and thunder and the fight outside.

Hours pass. Eventually, Max is gone. She must have snatched her handbag and stumbled away in her heels, blonde and bleary-eyed. I rise, to emerge and greet the blinding sun outside. And now the scenes there aren't violent anymore. They're just funny.

It's 1742 and a bunch of drunken Scottish bastards are sprawled out on the grass. Most of them are wearing brown and faded-red tartan, and the village stands just behind them. Every last one of them is absolutely wasted. One or two are still able to stand— McGlover is one. He staggers round in circles, a mead horn in one hand and half a bagpipe in the other. He's trying to remember where he left his wife, but realises he can't remember which town he's in. Meanwhile, Proinsias Mac Hardunit is doing the most lame-ass walk I've ever seen, clutching his spear and holding it up in homage to the pagan god Wankup. He's yelling a bunch of incomprehensible crap from Glesgae that even Liam from *Sweet Sixteen* couldn't match. And now there's a woman trying to be Boadicea, blue paint on her face and *far* too butch. She swings her staff about her, thwacking some of the invalids lying on the deck (if she isn't kicking and swearing at them as she passes). They yelp in pain, but they don't get up, going straight back to sleep after fourteen pints o' the black. "*ALBA GU BRÀTH!!*" is the patriotic growl-cry from McDougal who's just appeared through the fog in the distance. Wannabe Boudicca spins round, glares at him with a dumb, low-IQ look, then shakes her head and goes to kick the next drunk ass in the groin. Her boot comes off and narrowly misses a sheep grazing nearby.

At that moment, Lin woke up.

Now fully awake, she lay in bed, laughing almost uncontrollably to begin with. Presently, she took a moment to catch her breath, which wasn't easy as she continued to giggle regularly over the next three minutes.

Wow, that was sick! she exulted. Though she would dream often, usually twice a week, to wake smiling or laughing from a dream was rare. A precious, delicious rarity that Lin could count on one hand. As she gathered the bed covers to herself, she smiled in warm gratitude for the folk music that had entered her life a year ago. A quieter genre it may have been, but man, it was worth it. Just as fun to play as post-hardcore, with less drum equipment to haul around at gigs, and the imagery and culture around the music were vibrant, a rich and iconic source. She loved it.

"Man, what a feckin' dream!" she finally said aloud to the otherwise empty room. Though having just woken, her next decision was one of determination. "Right, I'm writin' that down. No doubt about it." She sighed, swiped her fringe from her eyes and pulled herself out of bed, feeling her way round to the door. Flicking the living room light on, she saw the neon digits on the microwave standing at *04:31*. She grabbed the nearest sheet of paper and, using a pen, sat at the kitchen table to scribble down what she could remember, vague though it already was.

Once more or less satisfied, she put the light back out on her way to the bathroom. As she used the toilet she thought again of Maxine, her one-time physio for a minor shoulder injury. Maxine had, without a doubt, been gay, but she had probably never worn leather, let alone breached professional standards. *Good dream score though, baby*, Lin thought to herself, smirking briefly.

Upon heading back to bed, she suddenly recalled Josefine as well. And with it, the song. A catchy melody it had been—and yes, it *was* Josefine Dahl who'd been singing it. *Thanks, Jo. I owe ya one.* She sighed, returned to the kitchen, and took it down note for note before she could forget it. It had been in C major, so she quietly hummed "do, re, mi, fa, sol" to herself for guidance. She found—and this had happened before with her dreams—that she could remember the tune with relative ease. The lyrics, for the most part, had also remained fresh.

PART TWO

Stumbling Blocks

CAIBIDEIL A TRÌ
CHAPTER THREE

Pessimism

Mar 3rd, Young Street, North End

"One medium latte?"

The recipient looked up from his notebook. "Thanks."

"You're welcome. Enjoy!"

The Fat Cat was a little busier than was customary for a Sunday afternoon, due in part to the unrelenting rain outside. Yet the background din was not distracting as Herman sat, looking after the band's Internet presence. Having assumed this responsibility soon after joining Skylight on lead guitar, his efforts to further his knowledge of social media and website optimisation had intensified since the band's shift to folk music. Unfortunately, the task he was currently engrossed in made little use of any learning, be it his own or that of the imbeciles he was dealing with.

In the last 24 hours, the band had received eleven comments on four of their music videos, which was more than they were used to getting. Initially excited, Herman had been in for an unpleasant surprise. The first three comments were from a user with the pseudonym *eireboi* (*eire* denoting Ireland, *boi* a male of some age).

> *terrible. Cant understand a shit ur singin so give up now ÉIRINN GO BRÁGH*

> *play ur own music. feckin yanks your just as retarded as you sound*

The third comment was about a set of jigs that the band actually had composed:

> *stop it STOP IT leave our music alone, yankee blood cant bring it Is treise an dúchas ná an oiliúint*

The catalogue of errors in this highly valuable feedback was, on its own, stupefying. Poor spelling and grammar on all accounts, racist abuse levelled at a band that wasn't even American to start with, and— for one seemingly so proud of his Irish heritage—an inability to spell *bragh* in its correct Gaelic form. The man, if a grown man at all, either had the IQ of a toilet brush or his priority was not accuracy, just to trigger people. *Probably both*, Herman had thought heatedly. As someone who had always cared deeply about his artistic output, Herman's first intention had been to try and reason with this halfwit, or to counter the Irish equivalent of *a leopard cannot change its spots* with a German rendering of *piss off.* Having taken a moment to calm down, he was now opting to bite the bullet, blocking the user from the band's channel and reporting him to the hosting site's moderators. He included a brief message within the 250-character limit.

> *Dear admin, I'm reporting this user because he violates your site's guidelines. He is writing racist, insulting and provoking comments on my band's music videos. He is clearly a troll. Below you'll find some links. Please remove the user. Thank you!*

Herman sent it. The mods would take a look into it. Whether they would ban *eireboi* was a different matter; Herman had once reported another user for mouthing off at the band (albeit with more profanity than patriotic rhetoric) and refusing to stop when asked politely. The mods had replied in dry, uninspired terms that they had found "no evidence" of a contravention of their terms of use.

Well, whatever, Herman tried to dismiss it as he clicked the Back button. Next up were several comments by a second user; Herman needed only to read the username to know that these, too, were not going to be serious. How the smut filters had missed the pseudonym *anal poo* was beyond him. The only good thing about this user's "input" was that none of it was aimed directly at the band.

Worship the Lord Almighty your God and ye shaltbe spared the ravages of syphilis. For Jesus gave us not the spirit of Satan, but of charity and a pact of cum. (Romans 92:3–4)

by byye ~~byeeeeeeeye~~–beyee ~~byeeeee~~ eee ebe ~~byé éeéeye eye~~ beebeeyebee .–..

[a string of over twenty emoticons chosen at random]

By then the light beam cloud in a ball schoolpark with oily men floating into tree witchs smileing as they phlap and melt heads mmmMMMMMMMllmhhmmhmhh o°^^–

Herman wondered what drugs this moron had been on while typing this crap. Though an atheist by choice, he would have wagered that Romans didn't extend to 92 chapters, let alone contain the dubious-looking quote. He clicked through the user's remaining comments (six in total) without reading them. Herman knew enough about trolls, scammers and other time-wasters to know not to "feed" them, but still his patience had worn thin. Hammering impatiently on the keys and cursing at his own misstrokes, he reported *anal poo*. Surely he hadn't been alone in so doing. But would anything come of it? *Even if he gets banned*, Herman thought bleakly, *he'll probably just create a new account.*

Of the two unread comments that remained, thankfully the first was genuine. A thumbs-up from a friend on "Llifogydd Capel Celyn", another of the band's self-penned instrumentals. *Sounds great guys.*

Keep up the good work! The friend, Cody, might not have been aware that Gus and Herman had written the dramatic piece about the 1965 destruction of one of Wales's last monoglot, Welsh-speaking villages, but his words were still a breath of fresh air. The final comment, meanwhile, was a parting shot from *eireboi*, and the lowest of all his contributions. It contained a blatantly xenophobic reference to their accordionist Rashesh's Indian roots.

With no desire to read it twice, Herman closed the notifications window. Shaking his head and exhaling in irritation, he could not help that his first thought was in his native German. *Also ehrlich...wenn sie DAS nicht entfernen, dann stimmt was nicht.* In emotional terms, this translated roughly as *I'm very tempted to put our videos up elsewhere.*

Sitting back in his café chair, he wondered what may have caused the sudden deluge of negative and insincere comments. Had these two users been working in concert? Were they targeting people arbitrarily and seeing who would rise to the bait? Maybe it had been someone's idea of a joke at a drunken party. Whatever the case, it was annoying. *If this is some kind of sign that our videos are performing well*, Herman mused, *then it doesn't feel like it.*

He minimised his browser and took a sip of his coffee, which was still warm. The pessimism was starting to set in as his frustration turned to resentment. *The mods don't care*, he vented to himself. *They don't protect the people who use their site. Why don't they do their job properly? If no-one gets punished, the trolls can just do what they want.*

As he went on, his objectivity paled further. Was *that* why their videos were having trouble cracking 1,000 views? Did the site think they were boring, and so refused to promote them effectively? "Folk's not cool," was how some cocky, know-it-all teen walking past one of their gigs had put it. Was he right after all? Did you have to resort to making shallow, superficial pop videos or leaving stupid, semi-relevant comments in order to get other people's attention? Was *that* what it would take for the band to get enough views, likes and subscribers to get paid anything at all through this site?

Shitty algorithms, he thought angrily. He hated them. They changed on a whim, mechanically homing in on the 1% of sugar-coated "talent" out there and leaving the other 99% of hardworking artists to struggle. To go without. *It's just hopeless.*

For five minutes he sat, arms folded, staring vacantly into space. If any of the customers or staff near him were picking up on his mood, he didn't especially care. He took the occasional sip of his drink, perhaps to reassure the world that he wasn't actually mad. But yet again, it all seemed pointless. *Hi, I'm Benjamin Wieske. My musical friends call me Herman. I work thirty hours a week so I have more time for my music.* Yeah, sure. And how much was he making out of his precious, beloved music? *Not enough to earn a living.* Make that *not enough by far.*

What helped pull Herman out of his present rumination was that he needed a pee break. He exhaled, made the effort to lock his notebook, and got to his feet. Sighing again, he headed for the stairs as the strains of chillout jazz droned on over the café's speakers. At least the Cat's staff could be relied upon to keep an eye on his belongings. By the time he was done, he felt a little better, a little less despondent. He returned to the table, tying his shoulder-length hair back and hoping in spite of himself that someone had not, in fact, walked off with his laptop. It was still there, waiting in standby for him.

Retaking his seat, a positive thought popped into his mind then. It was a nice laptop, to be perfectly fair. He went to open it, but a different idea came to him; he took his phone out and posted in the band's group chat instead.

I've put more than ten hours into it this week. I don't get it. Faith Kirkland says to stay strong during the hard times, but I don't feel strong right now. Hope I don't ruin anyone's day.

Once he'd written the full message and sent it, he unlocked his notebook. Taking one last look at the band's video profile (there were no other new notifications), he shook his head again, then closed the tab. On the band's other social media channels, today's and yesterday's efforts had brought in a small number of likes, hearts and supportive comments. But as usual, their feeds were dominated primarily by posts about free webinars, paid self-development courses, consumer products that he didn't especially care for, inspirational quotes, semi-humorous memes, selfie videos, and meaningless messages about whose dog had chased the cat around the garden, whose two-year-old had used a "big word" or whose head a pigeon had taken a crap on. One thing that did bring a brief smile to Herman's face was an image of a turtle, carrying a Great Highland bagpipe and a barrel of Scotch on its back. For all the other junk and clutter, *that* was cute.

Herman finished most of his latte, mainly to avoid drinking it cold. Even with his best attempts to crack the social media sites, he still feared that much of it was down to guesswork, to pure luck. Some of the band's recent content had received little interest from anyone, no matter how creative or meticulous he had been. Even posts about St. Patrick's Day (the parade through Downtown was now just a week away) had been flatlining, generating a mere handful of click-throughs on their respective CTAs (calls-to-action). Meanwhile, a cursory share of a message, image or video that, to Herman's mind, did nothing to stand out from the rest, would rack up views in the hundreds and reactions into double figures. He thought again of his thirty-hour employment contract, and the time he'd been consistently pouring into the algorithms lately. Into trying to understand them, to milk them and reap the benefits. And ultimately settling on a heuristic, let's-try-this-and-see-if-it-flies approach. Maintaining belief in the quest was tough.

Fortunately, one who unfailingly believed in him was Ailish. Herman pictured her smile, and heard her reassuring voice in his head. *You'll get there, honey. Just give it time.* That always helped. He hoped she was right. At least she allowed him the time and space he needed for the band, that was one worry less. Being the artist he was, Herman had even woven that factor into one particularly important conversation back in November.

Herman: "Sweetie, does it bother you that I don't earn as much as you?"

Ailish: "No. Why would it?"

Herman: "And will it ever bother you?"

Ailish: *[laughing]* "Of course not, honey."

Herman: *[producing the ring]* "Well then, I'd like to ask you something."

He smiled in fond recollection of that moment in front of Toronto's Scotiabank Arena (home of course to the Maple Leafs). Then, with an effort, he gathered his motivation and moved onto the next task, which was streaming. Today's learning had revolved further around the goal of earning more revenue from the music streaming sites. "To get your music on playlists generated by other users, you need to reach out to them," had been Faith Kirkland's exact words. Following the teachings of his impeccable online mentor, Herman had been researching playlists and compiling a list of those that featured folk or punk bands. Quite a few of them were artists he enjoyed listening to himself. The next step was to target the playlists' creators with personalised messages, expecting to be ignored by the vast majority but hoping for a positive reply or two, the few per cent who would take a chance on the band and add a song to one of their playlists. The theory was that, bit by bit, this would boost the band's revenue and exposure, while Herman could then try to build relationships with said creators—whoever and wherever they might be—and push for a little more of their promotional assistance.

His long fingers slid fluently over the keys as he worked. Though English was not his first language, Herman was a deft typist in either of his tongues. When growing up in Steyr, a small city 150km west of Vienna (and, coincidentally, only a two-hour drive from the Celtic Iron Age town of Hallstatt), he'd developed an early interest in the language of international communication. His teenage years spent dabbling in rock and metal music, electric guitars, Stanley Kubrick and Aleister Crowley—and, with friends, alcohol, nicotine and the occasional green bag—would eventually lead to a Bachelor's degree in English and American Studies at the age of 22. His course had included a year-long stint in Columbus, Ohio, an eye-opening experience for a small-town kid whose surname very few in the state capital had been able to pronounce accurately. After getting a job back in Steyr, he'd longed to return to the States, and had in fact paid one visit to his host family. It wasn't until he was headhunted by a Japanese company with a base in North America, however, that he would try his hand at living abroad permanently. "If I don't give it a go, I'll regret it later," he'd told their HR department. If his Bachelor's degree had put the young Benjamin on the road to *Herman*, emigrating to Ottawa had been the second step.

Though a period of adjustment, his first year of living in the Canadian capital had moulded him more into his present character. Having struggled with a sub-par work ethic during phases of his studies, his induction into an industrious, well-organised team had encouraged him to make some changes. To mature somewhat. It would pay off as the company kept him on and his salary went up a notch or two. Three years into his new life, he was invited to the cinema one evening by friends, and found himself connecting with a black-haired girl over a mutual interest in hockey, horror films, and exploring Ontario and Québec. One month and multiple dates later, he and Ailish Macdonald were an item.

As her name hinted, Ailish had made the comparatively short trek from Nova Scotia to the capital. "I was 21 and I needed an adventure," she'd told him. One day, said adventure would draw to an abrupt halt, as she received some sobering news. "They've diagnosed mum with CFS. Dad wants me to move back and help run the restaurant." A veritable curveball, but the pair discussed it, and quickly decided they were both going. "There were times when I thought I'd never leave Ottawa," he told her. "But as long as I'm with you...let's do it." Plus, Ailish's hometown was still much bigger than what he'd been used to growing up, offering the cosmopolitan pulse that had become a necessity in his life, but enough beautiful scenery to match.

In Halifax, Ailish's childhood friends had quickly grown to like him. And his English, which by now was near-native and an amusing cocktail of American and Canadian (Z was still *zee*, but *about* had given way to *aboot*). One of Ailish's chums was Tamila, a drummer by hobby, who would waste little time in snapping Benjamin up upon learning of his musical abilities. His promotion to the role of lead guitarist in her band Skylight would eventually serve as one reason for his resignation from his new job, as he took a calculated risk and went in search of some working hours more befitting his creative pursuits. For eighteen months now, since just after the band had changed its name for the first time (to Twilight Sky), he'd been with his present employer, working hours that freed up some welcome time and energy for his music. A passion that—so was the theory—would one day become a full-time gig, his primary source of income.

Herman had just messaged the third of his long list of streaming contacts, when his smartphone buzzed. He picked it up, to see a new message in the group chat. If ever you needed someone to obliterate the cobwebs of doubt with a verbal grenade, Gus was your man.

Bollocks to them, they're idiots. A bunch of keyboard-suckin pussies won't stop me.

Herman was surprised into a laugh. Like Lin, you could depend on Gus to give it to you straight. He remembered the respect he'd developed for both of them over time; that was, after his initial aversion to being re-christened *Herman the German* by the singer had passed. "*Herman the Austrian* just ain't got the same ring to it," their frontman had decreed one night after six beers and two shots of sambuca. Hell, only Gus could get away with nicknaming Tamila, his own cousin of 25 years, after the famous "Tam Lin" folk tune. And her response? "All right, fuck it. 'Lin' it is!" As such, *Herman* (missing second *n* notwithstanding) surely wasn't that bad, after all.

Smiling, and feeling some reassurance, he sent his reply.

Yeah. It's frustrating. But we gotta keep going.

The Rules of Society

Mar 8th, Brownlow Avenue, Dartmouth

"Yeah, but it's the rules of society, ain't it?" was Paul's retort.

"No, look man," Rash protested. Rather non-confrontational by nature, he kept going nonetheless, maybe because it was Paul he was talking to. "There's no one rule. It's not written anywhere that you *must* work in a certain role, or, *fulfil* a certain role in life."

"Works for most people though," Paul maintained his stride. "Look, some industries in the world are safe. Others are unsafe, unpredictable. You can't tell me that being a musician guarantees the paycheck."

Rash let out a breath; it was patience crossed with a little exasperation. "No, I suppose I can't," he conceded.

"Mmm, see what I mean?" Paul continued. His tone carried with it the usual hint of pomposity. "When you work for a company like this, you're guaranteed your money. Payday's every 24th of the month, without fail, y'know? I've been here three years and I've never been paid late. Never been *underpaid*, let alone paid late."

"Yeah, and you get your benefits," Steve added. "Pension, healthcare, all that." Steve was a diffident man in his mid-thirties, and when he did speak he would often concur with Paul. Possibly because his colleague, who sat next to him, had long since talked him to death.

"And tax as well," Paul himself resumed. "Don't have to worry about that either, that's deducted at source. No-one needs financial worries, y'know?"

"Yeah, but isn't that all a bit boring?" Rash challenged in the face of this pro-materialist logic.

"Why's it boring?" Janice jumped in. Behind her heavily applied makeup, her facial expression was one of confusion. "A job's a job. Get over it, Rash." Clearly she was unwilling, if not too unintelligent, to understand Rash's dissentient opinion.

"Yeah but, look," Rash tried to explain. He could feel the peer pressure as three pairs of eyes burned into him, but he persevered. "When you're a musician, or a writer, or *any* kind of artist, your future's not... mapped out in front of you, so to speak. I mean, sure, things are unpredict–"

"Yeah *and*, there are thousands of musicians out there tryin' to earn a living," Paul interrupted, stopping Rash before he could align all his thoughts, less still finish his sentence. "How do you know *your* band's gonna succeed? Big ocean, lots of fish, my friend." Paul nodded with raised eyebrows, as if his analogy were some golden nugget of wisdom.

"Yeah, but if everyone thought like that, *no-one* would try," Rash offered back. It was, to his mind, a weak and oft-quoted argument, but still better than none.

"It's not about trying," Paul insisted. "It's about luck. A lot of musicians get a record deal because of, y'know, right place, right time. Or they had the right ideas at the right time. *Or*, they had the contacts in the industry. Hard work doesn't count for much if you don't have any of that. A lot of people are naïve about it, y'know?"

"Yeah, you need luck, don't cha?" Janice agreed. Not that she would have known much about it. And of everything Paul had said, *naïve* left an especial sting.

"I mean, give you an example," Paul continued, not letting up. "When I used to do panto, I'd have liked to make a living out of that. But I knew it was never gonna happen. There's no money in that game, or if there is, all the big roles go to the big names, y'know? People in Toronto, Vancouver, Montréal, the major cities. And even some of those people struggle to get by, month for month. That's why I got a job here. It's obvious."

Unable to think freely in the face of Paul's verbal barrage, backed by his colleagues' herd mentality, Rash said nothing.

"I mean, yeah, some people in the company are bein' made redundant," Paul was saying. "Like what happened in Waterbury. But that was 'cause they became complacent, y'know? Dispensable. Shoulda worked harder, instead of waitin' for hometime every day."

How was it Nadine's fault she got made redundant? Rash thought. Not taken with Paul's arrogance, he expected someone to oppose him. To say, "Come on Paul, it's not that simple." Yet the only person who piped up was Rob.

"Talking o' hard work," their team leader broke in. He was peering over the top of his dual monitors, with something serious to say but a casual, I'm-too-cool-to-care smirk to go with it. "Are you two gonna keep flirting? Or are you actually gonna *do* some work? Paul, you've been on that email nearly eight minutes."

"Sorry Rob," Paul quipped as Janice started snickering. Paul looked round at her, his face having broken into the usual smug, I'm-a-funny-bastard-aren't-I grin. "Too busy daydreaming here." He turned back to Rash and quickly added, "no only joking, man." But Rash felt the implication behind his words.

Turning back to his own screens, he couldn't help but feel like a fool. Either he hadn't been able to make his point clear to his colleagues, or they simply didn't want to understand, and had closed ranks. Often, those who questioned conventional thinking were unpopular, a threat to the common order of things. An *inconvenience*.

To give the impression of being unfazed nonetheless, Rash rose from his seat and announced, "right, I'm gonna make some coffee." As he walked away he kept his ears pricked for another sardonic remark from Paul; but when his colleague did speak, it was only to ask Marcela if a certain Mr. Nazarin had called back yet. He'd finished his email and moved swiftly onwards, paying Rash and their discussion no further mind.

Rash entered the kitchen, and slid his cup onto the silver grille beneath the hot water tap. He flipped the lever and watched it fill, while in the background Janice was asking her voice assistant to stream her favourite playlist. Most of the songs on it were chart pop and R&B, music that could be fun to listen or dance to, but didn't offer much in the way of artistic talent. She would play it almost every day, but Rash usually tolerated it, as he had been raised to do. *Gus and Lin wouldn't be so kind*, he reflected now.

He had the kitchen to himself momentarily as he stirred in the coffee and some coconut milk, the latter of which he brought into work himself. He hadn't strictly planned on making another hot beverage, but strangely the kitchen felt like a place of temporary refuge, of quiet away from the noise. All that his colleagues had talked about this morning was celebrity gossip, the latest episode of their favourite reality TV show, overpriced concert tickets to see overrated musicians, and—of course—where they planned to "go drinking" at the weekend. To Rash, who observed a *straight edge* lifestyle (total abstinence from alcohol, smoking, and recreational drugs), the "go drinking" part was rather silly, a rebellion against nothing. And while he'd always known enough about celebs, TV and popular music to keep up with the chitchat, today for some reason it was all grating on him a little.

On the whole, Rashesh did not have difficult relations with his co-workers. Though he was not a practicing Jain himself (only his grandparents were devout), a core principle of Jainism was that of *anekāntavāda*. In a more contemporary sense, this could be taken to mean *open-mindedness*, and if all statements did indeed hold some degree of truth, then it followed that his colleagues deserved to be treated with tolerance and respect. The majority of them were, in fact, amiable. Only a handful irritated him; Paul was one of them, and today the vibe was strong. He liked the sound of his own voice, wore his black hair in a raised quiff that only served to accentuate his self-importance, and he was fond of straddling the divide between teasing and bullying whilst taking care not to explicitly cross it. When an important announcement went round via email, Paul nearly always made a point of notifying the entire team verbally, even though that was, if anything, the team leader's job. Was he angling for a promotion? Maybe. But even Rob had asked him before to temper his presumptuous behaviour.

Another one was Janice. Though no troublemaker, this woman could be stupid beyond belief. *Naïve*, to use Paul's word. For proof, one needed only to consider a [serious] question she had asked once. "Do cats really have nine lives?" Another beauty had been, "I buyed a new coat on Saturday." Even Steve had picked her up on that one. Rash hadn't been able to help his mental reaction, one roughly to the tune of *I think I need to get out of here.*

Those words remained on his mind for a moment as he put the coconut milk back and closed the fridge. He thought of the band, and tonight's gig at The Punch Bowl. Right now he wished he were playing with them. Sadly, as nice as the pub was, there was barely enough space on the stage for three musicians, let alone four. It paid more modestly, too, so Rash had unselfishly offered to sit such gigs out, with Herman deputising for him on sober driver duty. Instead, Rash had made plans to spend his Friday night with some old school friends; one of them, Jordan, played the saxophone but was more keen on sharing his stash of indie horror films with the group. Sometimes you were in luck and got a well-made, relatable one. Alas, Jordan's collection also extended to low-budget movies that suffered under poor acting, amateur props, and implausible (or in some cases, downright sickening) plots. Back in his teens, sitting up till four in the morning watching such entertainment had been something to do, something away from the parents. Now, he was approaching his mid-twenties; he was older, and seemed to be maturing at a quicker rate than some.

Grabbing his coffee and taking a sip, he returned to his desk. At least he would be seeing the band on Sunday, for the St. Patrick's Day parade that—in his view, somewhat peculiarly—was scheduled for a week before the actual day. And in the meantime, he had enough in his inbox and queues to get him through to 5pm and the well-earned weekend. Sitting down, he unlocked his PC and got back to it, answering customers and colleagues alike about items that were alternatively missing, incorrectly listed, or performing particularly well in the company's online catalogue. His teammates kept up their occasional smalltalk while the screens up on the wall (one per row) glared down at them, updating the numbers in realtime.

As he worked at a consistent rate and got through most of his coffee, Rash's thoughts returned once or twice to his earlier disagreement with Paul. His esteemed colleague certainly liked to pass himself off as a wise guy, a man well-versed in multiple faculties. But music? Was that really Paul's area of expertise? "We don't need a record deal to be successful," Rash remembered Herman telling him once. "Nowadays, nobody does." His Austrian bandmate had gone on to explain how the music industry was *dead*, with smart musicians opting for a do-it-yourself, online approach. Herman had most likely learned this from the lady whose course he was taking; Rash couldn't remember her name at present, but she was apparently doing things her own way, earning a nice living, and providing inspiration to fans and budding musicians alike. Herman, for one, seemed to put faith in her teaching. *Faith*, Rash noted then. *Yeah, that was it.*

But forenames aside, was a recording contract truly superfluous? If so, then Paul had been wrong. Maybe it wasn't all about luck, or being in the right place at the right time. And what else was it that he'd said? "It's the rules of society, man." Was that even a valid answer? Were there really a fixed few tried-and-tested paths that one could take in life? Or was Paul's comment more like an excuse? An excuse to defend convention and not bother exploring any alternatives?

Gradually, the clock approached 12:30pm, and his one-hour lunch break. By the time he was due to take it, the queues he was tasked with were looking tidier. Rob checked the rota and gave him permission to go, so Rash locked his workstation and walked away to retrieve his lunch from the fridge—Indian red lentil dal, no less. In the lunch room, which was just along the corridor, he was waiting for his food to warm up when Larry came in.

"Mr. Vasani, how's it goin'?" he greeted Rash. Larry worked in Sales and was a popular character, largely thanks to his good looks and sharp dress sense, but also because he genuinely seemed pleased to see others. He was also a devoted fan of Daft Punk, whose music Rash preferred to Janice's playlist.

"Not bad, Larry," Rash replied, with a smile. He motioned to the microwave. "Just heating my lunch up."

They chatted briefly about what Rash had brought in to eat; Larry had gone to the shop nearby for his usual panini. Rash asked him how his day was going.

"Ah, it's okay," he told him as he poured himself a glass of water. "Friday. Most people in weekend mode already."

"Yeah," Rash nodded. "I could use a weekend."

"Why, you in tomorrow then?" Larry asked.

"Oh no, I'm off," Rash said. "It's just that..."

Larry looked at him.

"Well, okay, keep this to yourself," Rash asked of him. "But I had a bit of a disagreement with my team earlier. Some of 'em, anyway. We don't always see eye to eye."

"Oh, in what way?" Larry wanted to know. An open-ended, salesman's question.

"Well, I don't know, it's weird," Rash said. "I won't say who it was, but some people appear to take offence to me being a musician."

Larry's expression turned to puzzlement. "A musician? What's wrong with that?"

"*Nothing*, right?" Rash stated firmly. "I think they get a bit jealous when I talk about, you know, being in a band, playing gigs, earning extra money with it."

"Oh, take no notice of 'em," Larry decided rightly with a shake of the head. "What's wrong with makin' some extra cash? I do that all the time. Not with music, but each to their own, I say." In the face of Paul's "big ocean, lots of fish" analogy, Larry's attitude was refreshing, not to mention spiritually restorative.

"Yeah, I wish more people saw it that way," Rash sighed. He then remembered his colleague's panini. "Anyway, I won't hold you up. Your food's gonna get cold."

"Alright man, thanks," Larry grinned. He grabbed his water, bade Rash a good weekend and headed out the door, presumably to take lunch at his desk.

Rash walked back and forth momentarily, mulling over what Larry had said. "Each to their own." As the microwave beeped, he realised his colleague was right. He took out his phone and wrote to the band.

Hey guys. Not in the mood for the films tonight. Mind if I come to the Punch Bowl and watch you guys play? I could use the good vibes.

He sent the message, then added an afterthought.

I'll even do all the driving. How about that?

He smiled. That way all three of them could have a Guinness.

PART THREE

Trial by Fire

CAIBIDEIL A CÒIG
CHAPTER FIVE

Degrading and Frightening

Mar 13ᵗʰ, Lacewood Terminal, Clayton Park West

Sunday had been fun. Hundreds of Haligonians had turned out for their city's Paddy's Day parade, many (including the band) sporting all manner of vibrant green—fun hats, long coats, garlands, knee-length socks and more. Parents and children had brought the Irish tricolour along, holding it before them as they walked, while others had picked a different Celtic flag, with Scotland, Wales, Brittany, the Isle of Man and—of course—Nova Scotia all represented. The band had been accompanied by Herman's fiancée Ailish, Gus's mum Alison, and Alison and Gus's dog Archie, as well as several decorated vehicles and a piping group playing just ahead of them. With the parade and St. Patrick's Day itself falling on separate Sundays this year, there was plenty of time to celebrate. And true to form, Gus had led by example, having one too many to drink at the after-party on the Waterfront and needing Herman to help him to the cab afterwards.

Practice last night had also gone well. The band had revised "Drunk On The Docks" and "Llifogydd Capel Celyn" multiple times, the former being their newest song, the latter featuring some unorthodox time signatures that Lin and Rash still found tricky in places. That aside, all four musicians had been in fine form and voice, with Gus remembering all of his lyrics this time (he'd forgotten a few at The Punch Bowl, ad-libbing his way round such moments with most of the audience none the wiser). The setlists they'd compiled for Paddy's weekend were sounding solid, boasting tunes (instrumental pieces), upfront rebel songs, explicit drinking songs, more introspective numbers and a few romantic ballads. One more run-through of everything on Friday, and they would be set. Minus the occasional exception, rehearsals took place in the shed that Ailish's parents had generously purchased, installed and soundproofed for them at the far end of their garden.

At present, Lin was standing in line at Lacewood Terminal. She was dressed in her black Doc Martens, navy blue jeans that were ripped in places, a dark grey sweatshirt, and the black leather jacket and toque (or beanie, as it was otherwise known) that were good for keeping out the cold of early spring. She was waiting in the drizzle to board the number 39 bus that she'd changed from the 10 for. A pleasant ride home, however, was most likely out of the question as she would be sharing the bus with the same three youngsters who'd tested the passengers' nerves on the 10 with their loutish conduct. This had included spraying deodorant for all to smell (read: choke upon). Lin guessed that they were in their late teens. While she considered herself a tolerant individual, she had quickly grown tired of the loud, profanity-laden conversation of these red-blooded young men. It had been all about women, being unemployed, reality TV, women, getting into violent confrontations (and then trouble with the police), binge drinking, and back round to women again. *They're probably all virgins*, Lin had thought derisively. She remembered how, on a trip round the British Isles last summer, she'd taken several double-decker buses through London. *We could use more of them here*, she reflected now. *That way these twats could sit up top, and everyone else might get some peace.*

Two of the gentlemen in question were finishing their cigarettes prior to boarding the bus, stamping the ends into the ground instead of stubbing them out and disposing responsibly of them. Lin herself had been nicotine-free today, partly as she'd smoked and vaped too much at The Punch Bowl, proceeding to regret it the next morning. Admittedly, this excessive consumption occurred at most gigs she played or watched, and St. Patrick's weekend would likely be no exception. On Saturday the band was at—*ha-ha*—The Smoke, supporting native Dubliner David Lannon and his band, who'd apparently won a few folk awards. Sunday would be equally exciting, with the band making the long journey to the yet-uncharted Sydney for their first show on Cape Breton Island, and the main support slot to boot. Lin knew what time they needed to arrive at The Cannon (being the venue), who to talk to (a rather sullen barmaid called Lauren), how long they were playing for, and how much they were getting paid. These details were her responsibility as the band's booking agent and unofficial spokeswoman, though Gus had split the task with her back in the Skylight/Twilight Sky days. "He'd be too drunk to do it these days," Lin had recently joked to Ailish.

She showed her ticket to the driver, and took a seat in the mid-section of the bus; the three chumps ahead of her had gone to the very back. *It's where the cool kids sit*, she thought satirically. She put her Bluetooth headphones (the in-ear kind) back in, took her phone out and tuned back into The Acoustic Outpost. A nice radio station based across the water in New Hampshire, it was currently broadcasting a sweet little number by Emma Stevens, herself a Cape Bretoner, and one who sang in English and Mi'kmaq. The latter language was indigenous to the Atlantic provinces, and fundamental to a culture that Lin bore some interest in and had been meaning to look into.

The bus started to pull away. On most days, Lin had no need of public transport, as she would take her second-hand but ever-reliable Honda into work and back. Today, she'd hitched a ride with her mum, so she could have a drink with Danny and Caleb in the evening, which had been pleasant. Mum worked for a bank in Downtown, Lin was part-time as a barista in an artsy West End café where, for now at least, she was content. Better off in any case than she'd been in her previous [forty-hour] job, an office-based customer support role that had paid better, but entailed working for a dull and unaccommodating woman with whom she had ultimately fallen out.

It was nine stops to home, which was a two-bedroom apartment that Lin and her mum Jean had originally moved into eight years ago, after the divorce. "Your father's been having an affair. With two other women." Words indelibly stamped upon Lin's memory. It had been a tough time for mother and daughter, one that had tested and strengthened their bond. Alas, with a lesser combined income, it had made little sense to continue renting the condo. Finances were more stable now that Mark was on the scene; a painter and decorator by trade, he was a relatively quiet man, and not much of a music enthusiast, but he did seem to care for Lin's mum. For the moment, though, there were no plans to upscale their living conditions. In truth, their second-floor apartment was nice, and it offered just enough space for three people. But it wouldn't have hurt some of the other tenants to take more pride in the building and its communal facilities, nor the management company to do something about their laziness.

The bus had gone almost three stops, with Lin managing to enjoy the music over the *whirr* of the vehicle, when a plastic Coca-Cola bottle came sliding past her along the aisle. A third or so full, she recognised it as belonging to one of the young men at the back. He'd been swigging from it back at Lacewood; now he'd seen fit to launch it down the bus. Right on cue, there were audible guffaws from the other two.

Lin felt a stab of annoyance, but chose to ignore it. Looking out of the window in an attempt to distract herself, she saw how the rain was coming down more heavily now. It pattered softly against the windows of the bus, which were already a little misted. Outside it was 3°C, or at least that was what her phone had just confirmed. She turned the music up slightly, a notch louder than was usually comfortable, and started drawing a non-specific doodle on the windowpane with her right index finger. *Choose art, not war*, was the saying that came to mind. She smiled briefly at that. Her fingernails were currently unpainted, but she would be sure to sort that out before Saturday's perfor–

The second bottle came flying past her as the bus passed Bethany Way. This one was empty, and it clattered around the deck on its way to the front of the bus. Her patience fraying, she pulled her earbuds out, turned and gave the three brats a disapproving look. One reacted by pulling his hoodie up over his head, in a mock attempt to hide, while the other two—probably the same ones as before—saw her and started cackling again. It was a maddening, low-IQ laugh, as if to them their behaviour was hilariously entertaining.

At that moment, the driver also reacted; he put the brakes back on, having just moved off from the previous stop. Lin turned back to the front, as the men behind her swore excitedly over the mechanical beats that hissed from one of their phones. The driver, a grey-haired man with glasses who looked about sixty, poked his head round the corner and asked the three of them to knock it off. It was too polite. One of the three mockingly parroted the driver's words, and his less-debased accent, as he drove on. Lin wished he would stop the bus altogether and throw these idiots off, along with their stupid gangsta hip hop (or whatever it was) and fizzy drinks bottles. Lin understood that they probably came from deprived backgrounds, and uncaring families, but *two* bus journeys of it was too much. None of the remaining passengers on the 39, being two older women in front of Lin and a thirtysomething man to the side, stirred. Either they were oblivious to the situation, or simply reluctant to pipe up, hoping that the youths would quieten down.

Like that time on North Street, Lin thought then, putting her cans back in. The music couldn't stop her from revisiting the scene. A rainy evening last autumn. Waiting again for the bus, along with half a dozen other passengers. Among them a vile, aggressive little man, standing there, talking right into his girlfriend's face, relentlessly berating her in a language Lin couldn't identify. The poor woman sobbing, visibly frightened, the toddler in her arms blissfully unaware of any of it. Nobody else bothering, or brave enough, to come to their aid. Lin had been about to open her mouth and order him to cut it out, when the bus had seen fit to show up. *Great fucking timing*. And had she boarded with them, to keep an eye on the woman and her daughter? No. *Because it wasn't my bus. I needed the 2, not the 5*. The feeling of selfishness, of *stupidity*, of bitterness and impotent rage (both at the man and the social-pussy bystanders) had remained with

Lin all evening. Culminating in a violent fantasy of completely demoralising this bastard, spiritually as well as physically. *You know what you are? You're a worthless piece of shit. That's all you are. That's all you'll ever be. Don't you fucking DARE knock her about when you get home. And if I ever—EVER!—catch you treating a woman like that again, next time I'll rip your cock off!*

Pushing it away for now, she counted the number of stops remaining. It was still five—five and a bit. She turned her attention back to her phone; unlocking it, one of the few notifications she had was from the band. Herman had been persevering with the social media, it seemed. She brought it up and saw that it was, indeed, another promotional post for St. Patrick's weekend. The picture of the band that Herman had retrieved and touched up was nice, one where Lin was actually happy with her own appearance. Rash looked every inch the charmer in his cream-coloured fedora, and Herman was as photogenic as always, the lucky *gobshite*. Gus, meanwhile, looked strikingly like a chubby version of Shane MacGowan. *That's where he puts the pints*, she thought to herself now, with a hint of a laugh.

All in all, they made a good team. The post was only a few minutes old, but had already garnered two or three likes. Lin wanted to leave a comment, but thought better of it; it wasn't always appropriate for musicians to comment on their own bands' posts. Instead, she switched to her browser, where the band's website was bookmarked. Standing out from the requisite contact and booking information, merchandise, tech rider, press kit and endorsements (the few the band had so far) was a similar announcement that Herman had put up in advance of Saturday and Sunday. *Four days till showtime*, Lin reflected, feeling excited. At that, she paused the radio stream and put some Shinrone on, being one of the bands that had played at last year's St. Patrick's party. Their "Moonglaze Set" started up in her cans as she put her phone away; the opening tune was an impressive number, written in 5/4 time and led by Nora's piano. Lin sat back and enjoyed the melody, but her enjoyment came to an abrupt end as a figure from behind jumped into the seat beside her.

She turned and sat upright. Yes, it was one of the men from the back; the same one who'd pretended to hide under his navy blue hoodie. He looked eighteen or nineteen, had a near-bald buzz haircut, and he stared directly at Lin with a smile she didn't like, and of whose meaning she was uncertain. Whatever was on his mind, it couldn't have been of much use to her. Now uncomfortable, she took her earphones out again.

"Can I help you?" she asked, dropping them to her chest.

"Nah," the young man said. The grin on his face remained. "Just admirin' the view." Behind him the others laughed hysterically. One of them called down to his friend, speaking in slang that Lin didn't fully understand.

She knew by now that she was dealing with a group of troublemakers, who might well try to chat her up. She could also tell from the breath on her unwanted neighbour that he'd been drinking more than just coke. She was about to ask him to go away; what stopped her was a sudden realisation that provoking him might be unwise, given his semi-drunken and testosterone-laden state. A few seconds later, he spoke again.

"What's your name?"

Again, she was hesitant to react. This was partly from a reluctance to answer, but it was also for another reason. Was she Tamila, her birthname? Or Lin, the one Gus had devised for her? She wished her relative were here right now—he wouldn't be taking any of this crap. In the end, her reply was rather tame. "What?"

"Your *name?*" the man replied, in a tone that made Lin feel stupid. "Don't you know your own name?" This prompted further laughter, a high five (or similar, Lin didn't turn around to see) and more incomprehensible gibberish from the other two. Again she wanted to tell him—*all* of them—to leave her alone, but the possibility that it might set them off (and together, they had her outnumbered) kept her from speaking. Perhaps her best option was to play along, to humour them and sit it out until her stop. Unhelpfully, none of the other passengers were making any attempt to get involved, nor even to turn round. *They're too scared*, Lin decided for sure.

"What ya listenin' to?" the man was asking her in the meantime. He pointed at Lin's earphones.

Lin was still uneasy, but gave a full answer. "Shinrone," she said. "Irish folk music."

"Irish *folk* music?" the man repeated, his face twisting into a confused expression. Then, it turned to mockery. "Ff-fuck that!" he scoffed. He turned back to his companions. "Ey yo! She listens to *Irish folk music!*" His emphasis on the final words underlined his ignorance of the genre.

Of course, the others thought it was hilarious. One of them broke into a derisive rendition of Ed Sheeran's "Shape Of You", banging a rhythm on the seat in front of him. Lin was made to feel as if *she* were the ridiculous one. *That's not even one of his Irish songs, you dickhead*, she thought heatedly.

The young man next to her then opted for another angle. One Lin could almost have seen coming.

"You got a boyfriend, darlin'?"

At that, she knew she had to speak up—even if she hadn't managed to stand up for a terrified woman and her little girl last October. With some of the no-nonsense attitude, she turned to face him.

"Look, I don't owe you any explanations. Leave me alone, please."

She crossed her arms and faced the front again. Her neighbour, whose pea-sized, alcohol-sodden brain was probably incapable of processing her words, turned back to his friends. He cursed and burst into laughter again. "*Ooooooooo-OOOOOOOOOO!*" came the sarcastic observation from one of the others. A part of Lin, the part that fear had not seized, was seething. *What's your problem? Not used to a woman with frizzy hair? A piercing and two flesh tunnels? A woman who doesn't like men, especially men like you who think they're so macho?* The rest of her simply wanted to get off this bus and go home.

The man shifted in his seat. Really, this was just an excuse to edge closer to Lin, which of course he did. His breath did not smell pleasant, and she didn't know what was coming next; an arm round her shoulder, a hand somewhere else or a remark about her sexuality, if this halfwit had even picked up on the fact. Actually, he had a different question loaded.

"Yo, where'd you get your hat?"

Lin was still unwilling to look him in the eye for very long. "Why?" she replied. Translated, this meant *It's none of your business and I'll wear what I like, so piss OFF.*

He licked his lips—not in sexual predation, Lin felt, but as a sign that he had more.

"Don't cha like showin' your hair?"

By now, she really had had enough. If carrying pepper spray was illegal in Canada, even for women, then threatening this prick and his associates with the driver and the police would have to do. But before she could say, or hardly do anything further, the man reached up, swiped her toque from her head and made for the back of the bus with it.

"HEY!" Lin sprang into life. It was a cry of indignation. She bounded into the aisle and mounted the two steps towards the group. "Give it back!"

The thief tossed her hat, which was made of hemp and had cost $25, to the one sitting at the back right (or the back left, as Lin looked). He, in turn, threw it across the bus to the third man. Twice more she insisted they give it back; it was no use with these morons, who were roaring with laughter.

Presently, the one at the back right rose from his seat. Composing himself, he slipped deftly past the one in the aisle, towards Lin. Dressed in regulation gymwear, he was at least four inches taller than her 5'6".

"Don't worry, babe," he said thickly through more than one missing tooth. "I'll look after your hair."

He then had the temerity to reach up with his left hand and start to stroke it, at the sides. Memories of tenth-grade bullying in the girls' changing room exploded in Lin's mind and heart.

"Leave me alone," she ordered him. Fighting tears now, she took a step back. "I'll call the police." The man, unperturbed by her warning, closed the gap and continued his chauvinistic behaviour, his face now six inches from hers.

"I said *FUCK OFF!*" Lin erupted. Her right fist came up, hard and high; it caught her harasser squarely on the nose. He uttered a cry and staggered backwards, past the one who'd taken a seat next to her. Falling to his knees with two hands to his face, he howled his head off, in a fashion not unlike his hyenic laughs. In the eyes of the other two, Lin saw entertainment turn to feral fury.

Hollering an expletive, the one who'd stolen her toque came for her. She raised both arms in a token block, but it was futile; the thug shoved her with a force that sent her tumbling backwards down the steps—and her heart into double time. She was lucky not to hit her head as she fell, instead catching her shoulder on the metallic frame of one of the seats. Pain shot through her right side; she shrieked and brought her left hand to the area of impact. As she did so, a kick from the same man went into her right thigh. Followed by another, which deadened it.

The man stood above Lin, bellowing at her, all of it unintelligible but for a series of degrading and frightening four-letter words. He was definitely aware of her sexual orientation now. Screaming, she attempted in vain to wriggle backwards, away from her attacker. Through the debilitating pain, she looked up, and saw him take a step back to generate a more powerful kick. *No*, Lin pleaded meekly, knowing he was going to break her leg.

At that moment, she got lucky. Her assailant lost his footing instead, partly due to the wet floor but mainly because the bus was turning—and yes, *slowing*. He landed on his back; the third man, who had come to join the assault, tried to stumble past him but tripped over. He fell almost head-first into Lin's calves.

As the new arrival writhed on the deck in an enraged, semi-inebriated attempt to pick himself up, Lin regained her courage, and had just enough time to kick her legs out from under him. Raising her uninjured arm, she grabbed onto the nearest seat and, with a surge of venom, yanked herself up. Her right thigh was completely numb, but she managed to keep her balance as the man before her got to his feet. For the moment, the other two were still down.

He's hit his head on the step, was the thought that flashed at lightning speed across Lin's mind, in reference to the one who'd pushed and kicked her. With a total disregard for chivalry, the one left standing now strode forward and pulled a punch. As he channelled power into his right arm, Lin's instincts beat him to it. Still holding onto the frame of the seat for leverage, she raised her good leg and kicked the man in the balls.

His knockout punch suddenly gone, he doubled over, cringing in much more agony than the one Lin had thumped on the nose. *Thank God for my Docs*, she thought bizarrely. Taking no chances, she threw an underarm swing—another of the moves she could remember from the women's self-defence course she'd taken in her teens. Her fist rammed into the man's cheekbone, narrowly missing the intended target. If last October on North Street had left her feeling powerless, tonight surely wouldn't.

The punch drew fresh pain from her shoulder, but it was effective. The man toppled backwards, landing again on top of his mate who still appeared to be dazed. The hair-stroker remained on the deck too, spitting mucus and blood as he cursed a great deal. With all three temporarily punished for what they had done, Lin did the only thing she could think of doing at that moment. The same as she'd done after finally giving Madison Dixon—the bullying, homophobic bitch—the same backfist treatment that day in November after school. She turned and bolted, making straight for the front door, paying no attention to the other bus passengers who were now goggling in disbelief.

It's shut, she realised with horror as she reached the front. The driver had parked the bus, stepped out from his seat and was, to his credit, visibly concerned for Lin's welfare.

"Open the door! *Please!*" she begged, pointing a frantic finger.

"Ma'am, don't you want me to call–" the driver started. Lin, turbocharged with adrenaline, cut him off.

"OPEN IT!" she screeched. "*NOW!*" Getting the police involved was not currently her main priority. Nor was politeness, and nor was her toque. All she wanted to do was get the hell out of there while she still could.

The driver obediently turned, bent around his seat and did what she had asked. The relief as the doors slid open was almost agonising. Lin glanced over her shoulder; the man with the nosebleed was still trying to help the other two to their feet. Better still, she saw that the other doors, which served the middle and back of the bus, had not opened. *Good move, driver.* And now the remaining passengers were backing away too, seeking strength in numbers at the front, and effectively blocking the men's escape. Lin felt guilty at the thought of leaving them and the driver to deal with these despicable human beings, but it was either that or risk further injury to herself. Who knew where they would stop if they got a second chance? What if they put her in hospital? What if they raped her? Or even kicked her to death? At that moment two words ignited in her mind, burning like bright neon lights. *Raymond Taavel.*

"Call the police!" she quickly instructed the driver. She pointed down the aisle to her aggressors. "If they come, kick 'em, throw things at 'em, don't stop!" She left anything else unsaid as she turned and leapt from the bus. She landed on the grass in the rain, and ran with all her might.

For two whole minutes she ploughed along the sidewalk, running as smoothly as her injuries would allow, and never once looking back. Her headphones, probably ruined by now, flapped behind her in the air, still held in place by the clothing clip at her neck. The downpour and chill headwind lashed ruthlessly at her face; several times she swiped water away in an effort to clear her vision.

As her breath started to run short, she began to lose speed. Now, she bitterly rued the day she had first entertained nicotine. Thanks to her stupid, cancer-feeding addiction, the men and the bus were now going to catch her. "*Please* let me make it home," she prayed under her breath. "I'll fucking quit, I promise."

Soon, though it had felt like an age, she came to the end of the park, and to within striking distance of Farnham Gate Road. Here, she allowed herself a brief look back, dreading what she might see coming down the road after her. Through the rain, there was nobody in the street as far as she could make out. Even the bus was no longer in sight.

"Oh, thank God for that," she gasped. But she wasn't safe yet. She put her head down and continued on.

A minute later and Tamila Ward was through the main doors of her apartment building, up the stairs, and behind her mum's front door. She locked it and stood in the safety of the hallway, panting over and over. She dared not turn on any lights, for fear that her attackers were still out there, looking for her. *Coming* for her. Alone in the darkness, she sank to the floor, raised her knees to her head, and let the tears go.

CAIBIDEIL A SIA
CHAPTER SIX

Why We Don't Walk Alone

Ross Street, Sherwood Heights

I get loud when I drink sometimes. Some people say I can't handle my drink. But I say it brings out the best in me. Just like the music does. Music and alcohol connect me with the human race. I read and hear about stuff that makes me sick, situations that would scare me shitless. But if music is escaping, then alcohol brings me back. It can bring ALL of us back together, smashing down the barriers we've put up between ~~ourselves~~ each other.

Some of our "traditions" are only celebrated (more like tolerated) because they've been tried and tested. Because 2000 years of life have led up to it. That's what the <u>mediocrity police</u> say anyway. But bollocks to them. I don't want to live by their rules, its (sic) boring. I don't wanna live life with no idea what I want. ~~Society's~~ Society wants you to think you're worthless, and that it's YOUR fault if you're unhappy. But I can see through that. I KNOW what my purpose in life is. I always did. And others do too. "If anyone's gonna make it as a musician, it's you Gus." That's what Rebecca said to me that time. Or there's Alex. "When I've had a bad day, I put Gus's band on." I won't forget that. It's the best feeling you can get, when people say your music's helped them. Just like it's helped me through the hard times. Tell me it's just a hobby? Well I wanna BE someone in life, change things up.

G us pulled up and sat back for a breather. By his reckoning it must have gone 2am, as the microwave had shown *01:46* when he'd poured his whiskey. Earlier that evening (the previous day now), he'd had a few beers with friends living over in Beechwood Park. After the taxi had taken him home in the rain, he'd collapsed onto the couch, mainly from fatigue and a little from the alcohol, and quickly fallen into the usual, semi-comfortable doze as the TV droned on in the background. After slowly stirring to smoke a Canadian Classic from the window, the worst of the rain now gone, his first resolution had been to continue with "Anthem For A Failing Angel", a ballad he was preparing for the band's second album, and whose development was charted upon one of the many scraps of paper adorning his vintage oak desk. However, the evening's conversation had inspired him to crack open the Bushmills 10 (purchased in person at the County Antrim distillery, no less), grab his current journal, and start a new entry.

Gus had never cared much for music streaming, largely due to the reluctance of the various platforms to pay musicians fairly. As such, he'd thrown on one of his favourite CDs; as well as helping to sustain the present mood, the songs were a good source of company. Also keeping Gus company was Archie, their Bernese mountain dog who'd followed him into his room and currently lay snoozing by the bed. Gus was an only child (a factor to which he sometimes attributed his creativity), and his mum worked nights in a call centre, so Archie was great for keeping isolation from the door. "'Cause of you, I can't smoke in the apartment," he'd once teased him. "But, you're family, so we'll say no more."

He rolled up the sleeves on his black cotton sweater. The heating was starting to kick in now as the four candles burned on, casting shapes that danced back and forth on the bedroom walls. Writing beside candlelight was a beautiful, eerie experience all but forgotten in the modern age, one that Gus enjoyed reviving if awake into the wee hours of the morning. Taking another sip of his whiskey, he picked up the pen and continued; his next line name-checked the Celtic punk legend whose abrasive vocals currently issued from the speakers.

What was it MacGowan said in that documentary?
He was talking about office jobs. "I'm nowhere now

and I'll be nowhere when I die" jobs. That's exactly how I feel. What's the point in getting up in the morning when your whole life's planned out ~~in~~ for you? When you got no say? Working in a music shop is actually <u>enjoyable</u>, and it gives me loads of spare time to do my dream. I don't care if it's "underpaid". I don't care if my grades were "disappointing" in school. I ain't thick. And it ain't just work, either. People go home in the evening, just to watch the same crap as everyone else on TV. They go out on dates, but realise they're not compatable (sic) with each other. It just makes you unhappy. And unhappy people don't find their potential. They won't make ~~moc~~ much difference to the world. It's like that American dude the other day who got yelled at by the bus driver, all for asking why he turned up late. "Change your job if you don't like it. Miserable bastard." Thing is, he was right. I LIKE my life and I like what I do.

To stand out in this world, you <u>need</u> to be different. A dreamer. A risk taker. In school the real reason they called me Gus was after Gus Wilson in Joby, that film from North England we saw. And it stuck. They always said I was a bit of a rascal. Now it's become my identity, and a <u>unique</u> one. Life needs structure, don't get me wrong. But it needs ~~free~~ individuals too. Lin gets that, she always did. I think Herman and Rash do too.

There's always gonna be people who don't get us. They don't understand us, they don't <u>wanna</u> understand. Ignoring them can be hard. When they suckerpunch the guts out of you, you can only hope it's the right *direction you'll stagger ~~in~~ on in. That's why we don't walk alone. It's so important to be around people who are <u>positive</u>. Who believe in you and what you do. And once success does come, like it's started to for us, you'll <u>never</u> make it if you don't BELIEVE and if you don't have others who believe in you too. That's how you live life on your own terms. A life that's actually leaves some kind of legacy behind.*

Even in his tipsy state, each word segued almost perfectly into the next, the thoughts flowing from mind to pen to paper. He paused again as the current CD track, a medley, reached the end of part one; two seconds later and "The Rocky Road To Dublin" kicked in. This song, and its rapid-fire lyrics, had hit Gus like a ton of bricks the first time he'd heard it at an O'Keefes gig. He stood up, and started whacking out the beat on an imaginary drum. As the tune built to fever pitch, assorted images filled his head; Lin thumping the bigger of her two bodhráns, people hopping and partner-dancing at last month's Smoke gig, fine-looking lasses outside afterwards with long hair and short skirts and loose-fitting tops. Even the oldies, who'd been dancing the céilí at the parade party last Sunday. Another flashback was to when he, Lin, her ex, and Herman had gone to see Celtic punk heroes The Tossers last year. *I wish I'd written this tune*, Gus cursed to himself with a grin. The medley reached its final part and he started to sing along, sipping his single malt in between times and not bothered if the neighbours could hear him.

Once it was over, he reached over the desk and turned the stereo system down for the moment.

Sitting back down to catch his breath, he pulled his sweater off, the T-shirt underneath it medium green with white stripes, and sporting a hole or two. As he flung the sweater onto the bed, he looked over at Archie; humorously, the 100lb Berner hadn't stirred an inch at his energised performance. *Wassup?* Gus thought, panting. *Too early in the morning for ya?* He smiled, feeling great.

"Failing Angel", the song he'd been working on, wouldn't be ready in time for Paddy's weekend. Nor would a new song that Lin had come up with, inspired by some dream she'd had recently. It didn't matter. The setlists they'd devised showcased the best of their work so far, the majority of it self-written, but a few cover songs and traditional pieces thrown in as well. Gus would have put it at roughly 70:30, a ratio somewhat unusual for the folk genre, where it was not uncommon for bands to forgo original material completely. "That's what happens when you start out playing post-hardcore," Gus had told Robbie from the O'Keefes once. It was true; nearly every band that Gus, Lin and Herman had played with in the old days had composed all of their own music, and as Skylight (and subsequently, Twilight Sky), they had done the same.

I still have that URGE to write. One day something's gonna show for it. Keep ~~did~~ digging away and <u>YOU WILL</u> <u>SHINE</u>. You can set yourself up, your own system, and suddenly people love you again cos you broke the cycle. THAT's how you grow stronger than the System we live in. I've sworn, and I still do, that I will hold music and integrity up higher than fame *and fortune. I promise I'll NEVER fall for any of that shit, I don't care who else has. There's only so much you can talk about money before it gets boring. With music, the right mood and that sense of <u>community</u>, we're GOD. Sorry, but that's how I feel. You can't feel that way when you're ~~obsessing~~ obsessed over something as stupid as money. Your destiny comes first, everything else follows. People just DON'T get that. Like my old man, he certainly didn't. Wouldn't have shacked up with that bitch lawyer otherwise.*

If we stay true to ourselves as a band, if we shine a light out into the world and see who shouts back, if the ones who ~~come~~ do can be trusted, if they stand by us, if we see through the bad deals and only pick the good ones, if we use our music to help other people and make a REAL difference to their lives, and if we stand up when we get beat down and keep walking, just <u>KEEP ON WALKING</u>...then we will get ~~we~~ what we want. The lives we want, the lives we always deserved. A life of <u>MUSIC</u>. Writing songs together, recording albums, doing interviews, playing big stages with big bands, and talking to people who actually give a shit about us. No more slaving to a bunch of rich pricks who just treat you like a robot and shove you in the garbage pile when it ~~soots~~ suits them.

This is MY LIFE. I'm gonna get what I want. And ~~I'll g~~ we'll get it <u>fair and square</u>. The more people ~~do~~ who believe in that, the better. It's a light of hope in a dark worl

At that very moment, a light on Gus's desk went off. He stopped scribbling and looked up—someone was calling him. *Eh? That's weird.* True, he hadn't been to bed yet and turned his phone off, but who the hell was calling him at this hour? *Maybe it's Mum,* he guessed. But she never called him at work, she always sent written messages. Through his foggy state, he became mildly concerned. Was everything okay? *Have the bastards fired her?* He discarded his pen, and as he reached for his phone he saw it was Jean, Lin's mum.

Auntie? What's going on? Again, Jean would hardly ever call Gus, as the two mainly communicated via text message. So why was she calling him at two in the morning? Even Lin had only ever done that once; drunk, on the way home from some party. *Maybe she's done it again and her battery's died,* Gus smirked to himself, as he took the call.

But as he heard his aunt's voice, curiously serious in tone, he knew that something wasn't right. Presently she put Lin on, and as his cousin started to talk, as he started to ask questions and she began to stammer in places, as he turned the music off completely and a measure of sobriety dawned upon him, he realised that Lin had been attacked.

CAIBIDEIL A SEACHD
CHAPTER SEVEN

Horror

Saturday March 16th (St. Patrick's weekend), The Bottle of Smoke

The pair writhed and thrashed, their hollering and howling matched only by the shocked cries around them. Herman had already dropped his C whistle and sprung from the stage to where Ailish stood, uninvolved and unharmed but still his first priority. Rash and Lin sprang from their stools and backed away, holding their instruments before them in mock protection. Seconds later one of the doormen, more stocky than his stage colleague, came ploughing through the crowd to assist the other four.

Gus had blood on his T-shirt as he looked back to the front-row faithful, wide-eyed and uselessly protesting his innocence as he was dragged backwards out of the pub and away.

25 MINUTES EARLIER

It wasn't long until showtime. The Smoke provided enough seating for just over a hundred people, but tonight the clientele already numbered 150. A good proportion of those in attendance were kitted out in the obligatory green; green T-shirts, bright green wigs, leprechaun costumes, green glasses of all shapes and sizes and, of course, green hats of all shapes and sizes. Splashes of white and orange, to complete the distinctive colours of the Irish flag, were also around. The band's own entourage had certainly turned up for the occasion; no less than two dozen of their friends had come down for the gig, including Ailish, Gracie (Ailish's elder sister), her husband Nestor, and Lin's friends Danny and Caleb. A confidence-booster if ever there were one. Lin's mum Jean, partner Mark, and a fishing buddy of his had checked in too, while unsurprisingly Lin's elder sister Charlotte had declined to show up. She was invited, but the siblings did not enjoy the best of relations. "Nothing ever bothers her," Lin had told Herman once. "She just throws money at it. Like when my parents broke up and she pissed off to L.A." Ailish's parents were working at the restaurant, while Rash's folks were away visiting friends up in Moncton, New Brunswick. Gus's mum

Alison, and a male co-worker of hers, had promised to come but were yet to arrive.

In the pub, things were off to a good start. Jason Girard, a solo artist renowned within the live music scene for his DIY approach to gigging, had played a strong half-hour set of acoustic covers. Minus one inebriate, who'd been repeatedly requesting "Wonderwall" by Oasis (while he wasn't bickering with some guy in the audience who denied knowing him), Girard had played to an obliging gathering as the pub had started to fill. It would be packed by the time headliner David Lannon was getting ready to take the stage. All performers had soundchecked in reverse order prior to the pub opening its doors to the *boom* of the noon gun; as such, the band would only require a quick "line check" before the first of their two thirty-minute sets.

With the noise of the evening in his ears and a Guinness (only his second) in hand, Herman was trying, without much success, to contain his excitement and slight concern as 7.45pm drew ever nearer. The dream of standing on a big stage, playing his heart out to hundreds or even thousands of adoring fans—a life-affirming feeling, to be sure—had been with him since his pre-adolescent years. As such, while tonight was still a pub gig, it was certainly a step in the right direction. The same would surely be true of the band's debut appearance in Sydney tomorrow. Earlier in the day, Herman had spoken to Rash of his incredulity at how, one year ago on this very night, he'd been attending his first ever folk gig. Within a comparatively short space of time, the four of them had come from nothing to playing the biggest gig of their lives so far, in any of the genres they'd dabbled in.

Through the thickening crowd, Herman could currently see the band's accordionist. Rash was dressed attractively in his fedora hat, matching cream jeans, and a crimson-coloured V-neck as he stood the far side of the door, chatting to a group of tourists. Lin was sitting at one of the tables outside, having a pre-performance chat with Ailish, Gracie and a few others. Only Gus was not accounted for, and this was the cause of Herman's concern. The frontman, who today was sporting one of the band's white T-shirts, had disappeared off the radar at 4pm and hadn't been back since. Lin had apparently messaged him twice to ask him where he was; the last Herman had heard, he still hadn't answered. But he was probably just having a drink with a few pals somewhere down the road, and Herman had every faith that he would be back for 7.35pm, as agreed, so the four of them could regroup and take account of everything before knocking the audience's ears into gear.

Meanwhile, over by the door, one of the [slightly drunk] Parisian backpackers that Rash was talking to continued in his efforts to teach him, and the other two, some rude phrases from his mother tongue.

"*Tu es une sous-merde*," he repeated.

"Okay, what does it mean?" Rash wanted to know, not attempting to pronounce it a second time; his French from junior high was not quite on par with that of Nova Scotia's Francophone community.

"It mean, *you're an undershit*," said the backpacker in his heavy accent. Rash and the others burst out laughing. "You say that, and all the people love you."

"That's jokes, man!" Rash cackled, patting the guy on the upper arm. "*Undershit.* I'll remember that one."

"Yeah man," the young man smiled broadly. "You say it to your friends, your girlfriend, your boss, the president of Canada. They love you forever, man."

"Alright, cool," Rash nodded. He didn't bother to point out that their president was actually a prime minister. Never mind the dodgy translation of *sous-merde*; a better rendering of the sentence would have been *you're a total piece of shit*.

Outside, Lin was still sitting at one of the collapsible tables with Ailish, Gracie, Nestor, and her friends Sam and Caleb (Caleb's partner Danny was currently making a call). The sun had slipped below the horizon, and twilight was almost upon Downtown. Smoking her second cigarette in half an hour despite her best efforts (and the vape pen in her jacket), Lin was catching the others up on the events of Wednesday night.

"Sorry guys, but we've got some *fucking* ignorant people in this world," she complained bitterly. "They think they can pick on people 'weaker' than them, or different from them. Sure, they're poor, I get it. They don't listen to folk music, that's fine. But that don't give 'em the right to stamp all over other people's feelings." She let out a snort of disgust. "Equality my ass. Ain't that supposed to be what this country stands for?"

"I know dude," Sam, who had known Lin since preschool, consoled her. "But there's lots of people out there who wouldn't dream of acting like that. I know how horrible it is when women are attacked, or victimised. I've been there. But I still prefer to believe most people out there are good. Harmless, at least."

"Well I wish they *all* were," Lin fumed. She picked at one of the rips in her jeans as she went on. "When we talked to the cops, I realised how lucky I was. My shoulder hurt like hell at the time—*and* afterwards—but it feels fine now. Alright enough to play the damn bodhrán, anyway. And the worst of the leg pain's gone, too. I mean, never mind missin' work. I came *so* close to missin' final practice yesterday 'cause of those dickheads."

"What, 'cause you were injured? Or were you too scared to go?" Caleb interjected.

"Both," Lin replied ardently. "You don't get attacked on a bus and then go out dancing, y'know?" She took another drag, blowing the smoke away from her friends. "I don't know. There were moments where I just wanted to cancel the whole weekend. Stay indoors. But everyone's been incredibly supportive. And I did feel better last night after practice." She took another quick puff. "I don't know, man. I didn't know *what* to feel. I mean, I felt stupid for lettin' 'em take my toque, y'know—not standin' up for myself more. But then, they were drunk, and I didn't wanna provoke 'em. And Mark said any one of 'em coulda been carrying a knife, or a gun. That didn't even occur to me at the time." She shook her head lightly. "I just wish I'd *said* I was gonna report it before I ran off. Said it to the bus driver, I mean. That woulda made it obvious that I was the victim, and not the offender."

"Hey, come on hon," Gracie reassured her, putting a hand on her forearm. "You've done nothing wrong, okay? They had no right to touch you. People like that are no-hopers, they'll never amount to anything. I don't think the police'll believe a word they say, especially given the witnesses. Every one of them defended you."

"Yeah, and like you just said, there's your toque," Ailish reminded her. "That'll test positive for fingerprints. No-one can argue with that."

"I know," Lin nodded, understanding. "I know. I just hope to hell it's enough." There was a good chance it would be. When Lin had gone to the police the morning after, she'd learned that all three delinquents had been pulled off the bus and arrested within minutes of the driver's 911 call. A huge relief, and an impressive response time. An ambulance had also turned up, with the men treated for injuries but none of them admitted to hospital. "A little more force and you'da broken that guy's nose," was the somewhat inappropriate comment from the officer Lin and her mum had dealt with. The same officer had not revealed how the offenders had been prevented from fleeing the bus themselves, but had alluded to the bravery of the driver and the other, non-violent passengers. The delinquents were currently being held pending multiple charges for public intoxication, theft (of Lin's toque) and at least two forms of assault. Unsurprisingly, two of them were already known to the police, for previous instances of intoxication, shoplifting, and—yes—assault causing bodily harm. Those two were nineteen, the age of majority in Nova Scotia; the one Lin had kicked in the *cojones* was a year younger. As for Lin herself, the Macdonald sisters had summed it up well—the driver and remaining passengers had all given statements describing her actions as self-defence. That was the other huge relief. Her toque was hard evidence now; tonight she was wearing a black Guinness cap in its place. Her Bluetooth headphones, meanwhile, miraculously still worked.

"Well, they shouldn't be allowed to get away with it," Lin affirmed. "It's still an insult. To art, music, call it what you want. We're beautiful people, in our own way. No-one should have to live in fear of morons like them." Staring sadly into space, she remembered April 2012 all too well. "Taavel. Poor bastard."

She took another drag, her cigarette nearly finished. Then, with some effort, she reassured herself. "Anyway, they're probably not gonna show up tonight. The gig should go to plan."

She was right about her first sentence. She didn't know then how wrong she was about the second.

Back inside, Rash ran the washroom tap and gave his hands a brisk rub. As he shook them off, Herman emerged from one of the cubicles.

"Hey buddy, what's up?" he greeted his bandmate. "You ready for this?"

"You bet," Rash grinned, moving over to the dryers. He raised his voice over the high-pitched whirr. "This'll be my biggest performance yet. My old piano teacher would be proud."

"Have you seen Gus?" Herman wanted to know, as he checked his hair (untied for tonight) and rolled one of his navy blue shirt sleeves up a little further. "We got just over ten minutes to go."

"Not yet, no," Rash replied. "He should be back in a minute. Well, he will be."

"Yeah," Herman nodded, still worried. "I mean, even if we start a few minutes late, I don't think the pub's gonna care."

The men walked out of the washroom just as someone broke into a loud, awful rendition of Oasis's "Wonderwall". Herman cast a cursory glance back; it was coming from one of the cubicles. Most likely it was the same guy who'd been badgering Jason Girard for the song during his set. Smirking, Herman followed Rash back into the pub, where the excitement of the room was palpable.

The pair spotted Cody, their friend who'd left the positive comment on the "Llifogydd" video. He'd brought his wife and a colleague with him; Jane, the latter, attended the band's gigs periodically. They greeted one another, and Herman made sure to thank them all for coming. A minute's conversation had passed, when Lin suddenly came up to them, needing to "steal" her bandmates for a second.

She took Herman and Rash aside, or as close to "aside" as a crowded pub might allow. In contrast to her usual vivacious manner before a gig, the look she wore was of disquiet. Herman asked her if everything was all right.

"No it ain't," she cursed under nicotine breath. "Have you seen Gus?" She gestured with her thumb to the door.

"Yeah I know, where is he?" Rash replied, checking his watch. "It's twenty-five to."

"No, he's outside," Lin told him, gesturing again. "He's had too much to drink."

"What?" Herman asked, after half a second's pause.

"*How* much?" Rash asked, nervously.

"Five pints and two shots."

"Sorry, what?!" Herman gasped, his eyes widening.

"Yeah!" Lin said gravely. "Him and his drinkin' buddies. They've *all* overdone it. Oh, I TOLD him not to hang out with Josh today! Why does he have to do this *now*, for Christ's sake?"

"Well...hold on," Rash struggled to think. "How bad is he? I mean, can he still play?"

At that moment, almost as if their accordionist had summoned it, four men came shambling in through the door, all wearing Guinness fun hats. The hats were not the problem; it was Paddy's weekend, and the band had decided against a strict dress code. What bothered the musicians was the state their frontman appeared to be in. Third in line, Gus stumbled as he followed his friends, almost losing his footing completely. Herman's heart suddenly felt like lead.

"There, see? He did that outside as well," Lin continued. She growled in frustration. "Arrrgh! I don't care if it *is* a drinkin' weekend. If he fucks this up, I'll kill him."

"Well...what are we gonna do?" Herman asked, looking to Lin for an answer.

"Well, wait a minute, calm down guys," Rash broke in again, the teetotaller playing the peacemaker. "There must be a way round this. Maybe he's still okay to play."

"Not like *that* he ain't, forget it," Lin insisted vehemently. She and Herman had played enough drunken gigs with Gus back in the Skylight days, and they both knew he'd passed the point at which his performance would become sloppy.

The trio stood, caught somewhere in a devilish triangle of confusion, contemplation and despair. For the moment, Gus remained out of earshot, his left arm slung around one of his companions' shoulders.

"Well look, let's at least ask him," Rash spoke up. He turned and headed for where the guitarist-vocalist stood. Lin and Herman had little choice but to follow.

"Hey Gus!" Rash called to him. Gus had his back turned and didn't hear him. Rash tried again; this time, Gus turned round.

"Yeah, what?" he asked. As Herman took in his semi-coherent state and smelt the booze on his breath, he realised Lin was indeed right. Gus was out of it.

"You alright buddy?" Herman asked him, trying not to sound too concerned.

Gus laid a heavy hand on his bandmate's shoulder. The three seconds he took to answer did nothing to dispel any of their concerns. "Dude, I'm *awesome*. This is gonna be the best St. Patrick's Day *ever!*" He adjusted his beer hat, seeming to have forgotten that March 17th wasn't actually until tomorrow. He then pointed a finger at Lin. "Only...lil' cous' here thinks I'm drunk. I ain't drunk." He shook his head repeatedly, looking about himself. "I ain't. I've only had...like, five pints, eh?"

He rambled on for a little longer, praising his drinking friends for being "so inspiring". While Herman and Rash exchanged a worried look or two, Lin chose to cut to the chase.

"Gus, drink water on stage," she interrupted him. "You've had too much."

"Eh?" was Gus's reply. He looked genuinely confused. Then, it turned to offence. "What you *talkin'* about?! I *ain't* 'ad too much to drink! I...I could always outdrink *you* anyway. You're a woman, you're younger 'an me. Shorter. That...th–"

"I'm serious, Guthrie," Lin stated icily. "We're on stage in five minutes. Don't fuck this up." She pointed the finger back for emphasis.

For a few seconds there was silence. Nothing but Gus staring at Lin, attempting to fathom her warning as she stood her ground. Eventually he just made a dismissive *pffffff* noise, lurched past them and headed for the washroom, almost walking straight into a customer—none other than Mr. *Wonderwall*—who was coming out.

"Oh God," was all Herman could say. "He's in a bad way."

"Told you," Lin grunted. She turned to Rash. "Still think he's good to go, do ya?"

Rash put his hands up in a *don't-blame-me* gesture, and looked away. Aware that it wasn't his fault, Lin retracted her curt tone and said, "sorry, I'm just *really* annoyed." Sighing, she then made more of an effort.

"Alright, look Rash—for what it's worth, I'm glad you're straight edge. Okay? It makes you reliable." She turned to Herman. "And you," she said to him. "What you did last night, checkin' up on me between songs, askin' if I was okay. Sayin' you'd have my back tonight. I appreciate that. All right?" Her words eased the gravity of the situation, if only minorly. "You're both reliable. Which is more than I can say for *him*." She pointed again, in the direction of the washroom. Neither Rash nor Herman replied, but both nodded in acknowledgment.

"Alright, listen up," Herman spoke next. If someone needed to be proactive, he was willing. "Here's what we do. We start the gig, we try one song, yeah? And if he screws it up, then...well..."

He hesitated for a moment, then made a decision.

"Then we ask him to sit the gig out, I guess," he finished.

"You mean play without him?" Rash asked. "Maybe...it would be better to cancel our performance?"

"Cancel the–?! You must be joking," Lin dismissed the idea. "We're on in a few minutes! They'll never invite us back if we do that. And I'm sorry Rash, but I ain't waited for today, done *all* that practice, AND dragged my ass through hell since Wednesday night, all for nothin'. No, we gotta do this."

"But who's gonna sing and play guitar?" Rash quizzed her, after processing her words.

"*I* will," Herman volunteered. "I haven't forgotten how to play guitar. And you guys can help me with the vocals. We can all sing, eh?"

"Yeah," Lin agreed, but she did not sound optimistic. "Oh, this is just *really stupid.*"

Cheers and whistles went up around the room as Martin, the head bartender for the night, killed the background music. Some of those standing at the back moved closer to the stage while Gus (now without beer hat) managed a passable introduction. "This song's for the pub. It's called 'Bottle of Smoke.'" On cue, Rash hammered out the intro to their Pogues cover.

Whether Gus would have made it through the first song without a hitch, the others never really found out.

Their opening number, and the dancing and clapping from the front row, was blighted at several points by the *thud-thud-thud* of a group of men seated behind the stage, banging their pint glasses loudly on their table. If their aim was to keep in time with the music, they failed miserably. To say that it made delivering a tight performance difficult was an understatement; Gus stopped singing three times, turning twice to yell at them to shut up, without especial success. There was a man on stage security, standing between the band and the crowd with no form of barrier to assist him. He disappeared round the side to warn the men off, but not before the song had ended.

During the band's second number, a set of polkas, unforced errors started to creep in. Lin's talking-to had left Gus in a sour mood, and he was unhappy at being made to drink water on stage. More pressingly, he was frequently hitting wrong chords, at one point playing muted strings to disguise the fact that he'd forgotten his parts entirely. Distracted by this, Herman and Rash both fluffed some of their notes. Lin felt unprofessional and let down, and she could tell by the way Ailish, her mum and other spectators were looking at one another that they knew something was wrong. But there was worse to come.

The band never managed to play "Cobbell Street", their first self-penned effort of the evening. Before Gus could attempt to announce the ballad— or, indeed, before Lin could get his attention and ask him to stand down—the same man from the audience started demanding "Wonderwall" yet again, in a dissonant, irritating drone. By now he was being a real nuisance, waving his beer glass in the air, with some of its contents going over the woman to his left. She and her partner promptly ordered the man to cut it out; strangely, the security man made no such motion. Nor did he issue a final warning to the party behind the stage when their banging, even with no accompanying music, resumed just then. As the drunkard started arguing with several of the audience, whingeing that he wasn't getting his favourite song, that everyone was *ignoring* him, Gus lost his patience. Unable to hear himself think, he pulled proceedings to an abrupt halt.

"Hey, will everybody shut up?"

It made no difference. The drunk, who hadn't even heard him, was still squabbling loudly with the couple that he'd managed to spill his Molson over.

"HEY, PRICK!" Gus barked down the mic at him, subtlety be damned. "*Shut the fuck up!*"

This time, the man heard every word. And that was all it took. In a second he went from nauseating drunk to enraged gorilla, barging past Lin's friend Sam and into the front row, mere metres from Gus. "*C'mon then, bring it!*" Now the security guard did step across and make a move to intercede, but he was too late. Without stopping to think—indeed, reflection was not currently his strong faculty—Gus whipped his guitar strap from his neck, and ditched the instrument. And then, in the most brainless moment of his musical career, the singer flung himself into the audience.

The security guard was unable to stop Gus as he landed clumsily in front of the heckler. He made a grab for his shirt collar, with the madcap half-intention of dragging him through the crowd and to the door.

The man, who outweighed Gus by twenty pounds, brushed his hands away and threw a punch, striking the frontman on the jaw.

Gus went reeling backwards, almost tumbling into his stage monitor but for the security man, who was there to break his fall. The drunk then came for him, yelling a series of F-bombs as surrounding attendees, many of them the band's own family and friends, screamed and backed off in horror. Thankfully two brave bystanders were quick off the mark, intervening and managing to restrain the attacker before he could reach Gus. A third man joined the security guard in prying the culprits apart.

The pair writhed and thrashed, their hollering and howling matched only by the shocked cries around them. Herman had already dropped his C whistle and sprung from the stage to where Ailish stood, uninvolved and unharmed but still his first priority. Rash and Lin sprang from their stools and backed away, holding their instruments before them in mock protection. Seconds later one of the doormen, more stocky than his stage colleague, came ploughing through the crowd to assist the other four. Gus had blood on his T-shirt as he looked back to the front-row faithful, wide-eyed and uselessly protesting his innocence as he was dragged backwards out of the pub and away.

As the door swung shut, Lin and Rash just stood gawking at each other, unable to believe what they had just seen. The atmosphere in the pub was destroyed. Herman, Nestor and several other male onlookers had their arms around their female counterparts, while one or two other couples were already heading for the door. Gus's abandoned guitar was feeding back; the soundman at the side of the room muted the channel as people brought their hands to their ears.

More critically, none of the band had any idea what was next for Gus. Was he being detained outside? Would he be let back in? Or shaken down and sent home? *Shit, they'll call the cops*, Lin feared. She wanted to make her way through the mob and see for herself, but then she caught sight of Martin. The head bartender was punching a number into the pub's phone—one visibly longer than three digits.

"Rash," she gasped to her bandmate. "They're calling Management. We're done."

"Oh no," was all Rash could say. He turned to her. "What do we do, Lin?"

Lin looked back to the bar. All the good times they'd had in The Smoke flashed before her eyes. The music, the bands, the drinking and dancing, the conversations and the camaraderie, the laughs, Paddy's Day last year—all of it could be for nothing. It was all about to be taken away; all for one stupid, drunken, irresponsible moment. Martin was waiting for Management to pick up the phone, his staff in disarray beneath the *ceud mìle fàilte* sign adorning the long wooden beam above the bar.

And as Lin saw those three words, clarity was upon her. Suddenly she knew *exactly* what she had to do. She didn't consider that the soundman may have muted the whole PA; nor did she care whether her spontaneous plan was "allowed" or not. All she could feel at that moment was the drum in her hands, all she could see was her vocal mic, standing before her. Almost *calling* her. It was *going* to be on, *damn it*.

Quickly, she removed her Guinness cap, tossed it aside and climbed back onto her stool, testing her instrument and mic quickly with a tap of the finger. They were still live. The maxim at the front of the percussionist's mind was simple, yet courageous. *I can change this.*

And then, in a clear, contralto voice, Lin began to sing the song that until that second was only known to her.

Low, low the river flows along the valley-o
Dry on dry, as it fails up the mountainside
General MacArthur's come home to see his sons
And if the circle goes five times around
There'll be whisky on the ground

To begin with there was no reaction from the audience, but as Lin entered the second verse, the uproar of the pub began to dissipate slightly. *See? I knew it!* This wasn't the first gig she'd played (or watched) where the woman in an otherwise all-male band would turn heads with a solo vocal. She sang the second verse, not caring to look in the direction of the soundman, who unbeknownst to her had very nearly chosen to kill the audio two lines into the song.

With her right hand, she started to grace the surface of her bodhrán. In no mood for any mistakes, her playing and singing were absolutely flawless. *I don't care if anyone attacks me*, she resolved. *I don't care about any of it. I am GOING to play this fucking song.* Rash put his accordion down gently and exited stage right; Lin was too lost in the moment to even notice.

In the face of her determined, yet ice-cool delivery, the din from the audience grew quieter still.

"Oh my God," was what Mark said to Lin's mum in the meantime.

"She's doing it! It's working!" Danny exulted to Caleb. In little more than thirty seconds, the pub had gone from unmanageable to almost completely silent.

As Lin approached the fourth verse, she looked over to Martin. He was watching just as attentively from the bar, the pub's phone now back in its charging station. With no idea of, nor concern for whether he'd spoken to the owners (or to anyone), Lin shouted two simple words in his direction. "Keep going!" And with that, she realised who she'd become. If only for a minute or two that night.

That's what Josefine always says in her videos, she reflected. *Keep going*. And the moment was like an epiphany. *I'm her. I'm Josefine Dahl.*

Armed with the confidence and inspiration of her German musical idol, she sang verse four of the five she'd prepared from her dream that Tuesday morning. As she did so, she kicked the tempo up a notch. Not once did she lose focus, not once did she stray from the key of C major, and all the while she rolled the tipper up and down the bodhrán, never tripping up in spite of some difficult triples thrown in there. A hesitant, but genuine whistle or two went up around the reassembled audience, as she cast her eyes back to the sign above the bar that meant *a hundred thousand welcomes*, and switched into Gaelic for the fifth verse.

Amidst a muttered "wow" from one spectator, she sang all four lines perfectly as she spied Herman out of the corner of her eye. She remembered now how her bandmate, who was standing to her left but had stood to the right in her dream, had corrected Josefine's translation of the word *othail*. *Sorry Jo. We outdid ya there, darlin'*. Smiling briefly to herself, she returned to the first verse to finish.

As the final instance of *ground* trailed off, Lin started to hit the drum faster. Then it was harder. The current in The Smoke approached ignition point as she forgot all about any residual pain in her right shoulder. Her playing became tribal, frantic, almost dizzying, like horse hooves pounding along a battlefield. From somewhere inside—she knew not where—there came a murmur. Then a growl. It built in ferocity, until seconds later the 25-year-old was screaming. An exorcistic, bloodcurdling scream from all the hurt and the sheer *injustice* of the past four days; the intimidation on the bus, the ensuing violence, the emotional and physical aftermath, the maltreatment of non-males and non-heterosexuals that was still too prevalent even in Canada—and now Gus, the damned idiot. Lin's final strike of the bodhrán was a thunderous hammerblow that overloaded the PA, and virtually levelled the pub.

As it faded to silence, for a second there was nothing from the shell-shocked audience. Then, the Irish pub exploded in a frenzy of cheers and applause.

Lin stayed where she was, head down, eyes closed and drawing in air, heaving as if she'd just run a sprint. Before her dozens of people were going bananas, all her friends and family clapping like crazy. She glanced up and out across the crowd, her emotions a surreal cocktail of grief and euphoria. As she raised a hand to wipe sweat from her forehead, she felt a presence at her left shoulder. It was Herman.

"Lin...*wow*! What the *hell* was that you just played?!"

Lin turned to him. She didn't smile. "I'll explain later. Come on, we gotta finish the gig." She pointed down to Gus's instrument—dented, but still functional. "Grab the guitar. Go! We'll deal with the rest later."

CAIBIDEIL A H-OCHD
CHAPTER EIGHT

They Don't Want Us

Sunday March 17th (St. Patrick's Day), Windsor Street, West End

We would like to apologise to everyone who attended our show last night. Drunken antics are normal on St. Patrick's weekend, but none of you came to see the violent scenes you witnessed. As a band, we do not encourage this kind of behaviour.

We would like to say thank you to the security team and the police for taking control. We would also like to say a big THANK YOU to the audience for staying

*with us, and The Bottle of Smoke for letting us finish
our sets. We hope that irresponsible behaviour will not
ruin the good reputation and cooperation that we and
the pub have always enjoyed.*

Happy St. Patrick's Day.

Kilmainen

"**O**kay so far?" Herman asked, having read the
statement aloud.

"Mm-hmm," Rash signalled agreement
from the driver's seat.

"Yeah," Lin, who had helped Herman compose it,
sighed mid-yawn.

The three of them were heading southeast, back
into Downtown. According to Rash's app, they were
five minutes from the police station on Gottingen
Street. The statement they had drafted had not yet
been sent to social media—it was incomplete until
more was known about Gus's situation. Was he going
to be released in time for them to get to Sydney?
If so, would the police allow him to play the show?
Would he even feel like performing at all? Whatever
the impending outcome, they had taken care to word
their statement so far as ambiguously as possible; the
last thing they needed was to dissuade other venues
from booking them, or indeed to put Sydney off
before tonight.

In similar fashion to Wednesday night, the
police had been swift to act after Gus and his

victim-turned-attacker had been hauled out of The Smoke. Having promptly arrived in a marked van and arrested the pair, the officers in attendance had read the culprits their rights and attempted to get information out of them, before moving on to statements from the security team and the civilians who'd assisted. Gracie had ventured outside to see what was happening, only to be told to go back in. The police had then spoken to Martin on behalf of the pub, as Lin, Herman and Rash had been able to see from the stage.

Come half-time, and the three musicians themselves were up. "We're really sorry about this." "We shouldn't have let him play at all." "That guy was heckling the first performer, too." Everything they could think of. By this time, a dejected but compliant Gus had been bundled into the back seat of the police van. Mr. Wonderwall, meanwhile, had been assigned to the cage, primarily to keep him and Gus apart, but also because he still wouldn't cease squirming and swearing. That aside, the only consolation was that the cops hadn't stopped the entire gig, given the lack of involvement of, or injuries to, the other musicians and revellers.

After the police had carted Gus off, the other three had used the remainder of their quarter-hour break (if anyone was even counting) to disappear around the corner for some much-needed breathing space. A chance to take stock of everything before the second set. Like the rest of the first, the half-hour had flown by, the band swapping two or three songs out where Herman was uncertain of the lyrics—or where the song was explicitly about getting drunk. Ultimately the trio had pulled it off, with any further mistakes of a minor and understandable nature. The audience had been kind, with several spectators praising Herman for stepping up to the plate on guitar and lead vocals. "You guys should play as a three-piece," a local man had suggested. "You don't need that other guy." The band had even managed to sell three CDs, despite Gus's early (not to mention flying) exit. Tragically, Gus's mum Alison and her colleague had turned up just after the restart, completely oblivious to any of what had happened. Cody's wife Liz had given them the full story.

"You really think they'll give us another chance?" Lin asked now. "At The Smoke." Not the first time she'd posed that question today; though in truth, it wasn't the most pressing of topics. Right now, their first priority was to Gus, and to learn the outcome of his arrest. While Lin's on-stage heroics might have turned last night around, none of it was of much help to their frontman at present.

"I don't know," Rash answered meanwhile, also yawning. He veered around a pothole, then indicated left. "We don't know if we're getting paid yet, either. All Martin said was that the owners had been informed, and they'll be making a decision soon."

"Great," Lin muttered, folding her arms.

"Well, it figures," Herman chipped in from the back. "If people start talkin' about this online, it's gonna bring the pub into...erm, you know, into..."

"Disrepute?" Rash finished for him.

"Yeah, that," Herman nodded. And then, a touch of dry humour. "Again what learned." Being a deliberately incorrect, word-for-word translation of *wieder was gelernt,* the German for *I've learned something new.*

"It ain't funny," Lin grunted now. "We're meant to be named after a jail. Not have our singer end up in one." She let out another yawn. "Man, I'm tired. I've barely slept, no thanks to him. He's lucky he's gettin' *any* of his weed back, I'm tellin' ya. I coulda gone through the whole fuckin' lot last night." Her bandmates, unimpressed, said nothing.

They drove the remaining distance in silence. Two roundabouts and a right turn later and Lin was reading the big, blue letters DAVID P. MCKINNON BUILDING for the second time in 72 hours. It would have been the third time, had Alison not called after the gig and told her niece not to bother going. She'd already made the trip herself, to learn that her son was being kept in overnight, partly to sober up ahead of further questioning and partly for his own well-being. Denied access to him, Alison's only comfort had been that, as the lesser of the two detainees, Gus had been spared the drunk tank and offered a cell with basic sleeping facilities. Upon learning of this, the rest of the band had packed everything up (including Gus's equipment and possessions) and headed home, to get what little sleep they might achieve in an utterly anti-climactic end to their St. Patrick's Saturday.

Rash parked up, creepily taking the same space that Lin's mum Jean had picked on Thursday. The three of them got out and made their way round to the entrance; on the approach, Lin puffed on her vape pen for self-composure, while Herman gave Citadel Hill a wistful glance and checked his smartwatch. It was 9am on the dot.

"Thanks again for last night," Rash said in the meantime. He was referring to Herman's offer to let him crash at the condo. "I was all right though. Sometimes it's nice to have my parents' place to myself. I just waited patiently for morning."

"We all did," Herman agreed.

At reception, there was an elderly gentleman being seen to by the lady behind the desk. When he was done, the three of them stepped up and asked for information on Gus. Lin identified herself as the arrestee's cousin.

"Mr. Ward is currently being questioned," the officer confirmed. "We kept him in overnight as he'd been drinking heavily, as you probably know. He's well enough this morning to answer any remaining questions."

"Okay. Are you able to tell us how long that might take?" Rash asked. As usual, he was doing a good job of staying calm. *Rational.*

"I'm afraid not," the policewoman replied. "I don't have access to the questions that still need asking, or permission to discuss the case. You're welcome to take a seat while you wait for Mr. Ward, though." Her conduct was professional, more so than that of the cop who'd assisted Lin and Jean on Thursday.

The three looked at each other, in a manner of asking *What now, then?* Lin turned back to the desk.

"Look, don't you have any idea?" she asked. She was straining to keep her voice pleasant. "How long does it normally take to deal with a drunk and disorderly?"

"That depends on the situation," the officer told her. "It differs from case to case." She tried to provide a useful guideline. "At a guess, he should be out in about half an hour. But we can't be held to that if he isn't, you understand."

Lin and the others stood awhile in thought. Eventually they thanked her and took a seat in the waiting area.

They'd waited just over twenty minutes, engaging in idle chitchat to pass the time, when Lin's phone rang. The caller was one she didn't recognise, though it was a local 902 number. She answered it; when you were the principal contact for a band (even one whose members were getting busted), you never knew who might be trying to reach you. Out of consideration for a man and two children who'd joined them in the waiting area, Lin took the call outside.

A mere thirty seconds later, she returned. Rash and Herman looked up, and knew immediately that something was wrong. Their percussionist looked crestfallen.

"Lin? Are you okay?" Rash asked her. He rose from his seat.

"Was that Gus?" Herman wanted to know, also getting up.

"No, it was Sydney," Lin uttered. Slowly she brought her blue eyes to theirs. "They've cancelled on us."

"What?!" Herman and Rash choked in unison.

"It was Lauren," she explained, pointing to her phone. "The barmaid at The Cannon. The stupid *bitch* has cancelled our slot!"

"Hey...wait!" Herman protested with his hands up. "What do you mean? Why?"

"She knows about last night!" Lin cried. "She said, 'we know what happened, so don't bother coming. We already found someone else.' Then she hung up on me!"

"Eh?!" Rash repeated, unable to believe it. "Wait a minute. *Why?* Is...is what happened yesterday really that bad?"

"Well *obviously*, if they think we're gonna cause trouble!" Lin snapped. She was conscious of the other visitors' concerned looks, and that swearing in Downtown's main police station would not be the smartest of ideas, especially not for the band right now. She managed to lower her voice. "Someone at The Smoke must've told 'em. You know what pub owners are like, stickin' together all the time!"

At that very moment—and the timing couldn't have been worse—the interior door went. Accompanied by a uniform, Gus entered the waiting area. Their frontman was not looking good. The blow to his jaw had left a bruise, still fresh and red. He looked tired, hungover, and his hair had certainly seen better days. The T-shirt bearing the band's logo in small, black letters still bore the bloodstains from the previous night.

"I'll show you out," the constable adressed all of them, leading them to the door. Only Rash dared to say a word; he asked Gus how he was. Unsettlingly, Gus didn't even look up, let alone answer.

"Good day now," was the impersonal goodbye from the uniform.

As the door clicked shut behind them, Lin immediately turned to Gus. "Down the stairs, round the corner. *Now.*"

The four of them got that far, before Lin let rip. She shoved her relative hard with both hands.

"Ya DICKHEAD! You've lost us the gig! Sydney's just cancelled!"

Gus kept his feet, but he stared at Lin with a species of incredulity. "What?!" he managed to get out.

"Whaddya mean, *what*?" Lin snarled. She spoke slowly, disparagingly. "Sydney...has *cancelled*...our *gig*!"

"They know about last night," Rash spoke quickly, his voice low. "They don't want us."

Gus's eyes and head sank, as the news began to register. Lin, with little time for compassion, pushed for a more substantial reaction.

"Well? What you got to say then? How about apologisin' for a start?!"

There was nothing from Gus. There remained about his person an absence that was disconcerting. With Lin crossing her arms and staring daggers at him, he finally looked up, but his speech was listless. "Just leave me alone."

"Sorry, *leave you alone*?" Lin hissed, arching two scornful eyebrows. "The fuck's the matter with you?"

"Tamila, calm down," Herman broke in then, using her real name for emphasis. He took her lightly by the arm. "Getting aggressive won't—"

"Get off me," she ordered him bluntly, batting his hand away. Perhaps a little residual trauma from Wednesday night. "I'm talkin' to *this* drunk ass." Herman stepped back, hurt.

"You've gone too far this time," she continued to Gus. She looked him up and down in disgust. "Thanks for ruinin' my weekend. Now *get in the car*."

She turned and marched off. Herman and Rash stayed put; the latter made another attempt to ask after Gus's welfare.

"Are you okay, man?"

Gus was staring blankly at the sidewalk. Slowly he turned to Rash, though still looking down rather than at him. "No," he said. He was monosyllabic, his voice uncharacteristically weak. "No, I ain't."

"What's up, buddy?" Herman tried to support his friend. "What's happened?"

Gus continued to stare into space, offering only an apathetic shrug of the shoulders.

"Gus, what's happened to you?" Rash pressed him, growing increasingly worried. "Did someone hurt you in there? Did someone *threaten* you?"

"Have you *taken* something, man?" Herman suspected. "Like a sedative?"

"Come on, I ain't waiting!" Lin yelled meanwhile. She had turned back to them, arms folded again.

A few more seconds passed, before Gus simply muttered a response.

"It was shit."

He then turned and slouched off in the other direction, walking away from his friends.

PART FOUR

The Outcome

CAIBIDEIL A NAOI
CHAPTER NINE

The Pain

He had been charged with one count of simple assault, and two counts of causing a disturbance (one for public intoxication, the other for obscene language). The result was a summons, requiring a return trip to the police station for fingerprinting and photography, followed by an appearance in court, where Gus would answer the charges. The immediate implication being, he needed to seek legal advice pretty damn quickly.

On the whole, the singer had been fortunate. It was his first real run-in with the law, which had helped mitigate the severity of the charges, as had his good behaviour following the arrest. In truth, the chances of Gus being deprived any further of his liberty were slim. Yet it was bad publicity for the pub, and it had wrecked a promising weekend for a band whose morale and reciprocal support were now in the gutter.

Having gone after Gus as he'd started to walk away, Lin had attempted, in her hot-headed, straight-talking state, to knock some sense into him. Gus, exhibiting further signs of apathy—signs indicative of depression, not sedation—had merely stated that he was "unhappy". With little understanding or empathy between the pair, the situation had then degenerated into a nasty argument. Though no stranger to drink herself, Lin had reiterated that Gus was a "drunken prick" and a "liability". Gus had responded by calling Lin an "arrogant bitch" who was "far too fucking aggressive". He'd also taken an unnecessary swipe at Rash and Herman, generalising that the two of them were "boring". Rash, amidst his ongoing efforts to keep the peace, had taken this to be a criticism of his healthy lifestyle. The most hurtful insult from Gus had been reserved for his cousin, in a haze of spite and self-pity. "If *your* life's so perfect, why'd you get molested by three men on a bus? I bet you *wanted* that to happen." That had brought an infuriated Lin to within an inch of hitting him.

To her credit, she had refrained, but her reply had been no less vicious. "Fine. Fuck your band. And fuck *you*. I don't want nothin' to do with you." Then she had walked away, this time without looking back.

That might have been the end of Kilmainen. Not to mention their relationship.

- RASH -

"Why don't you, Herman and Tamila—or *Lin*, as she calls herself—why don't you play as just the three of you? That Gus, he strikes me as unreliable. I've seen the likes of him before."

"I know mum, I have thought of that," Rash said. Both of his parents were on the line, with their son on loudspeaker. "It's funny, you know. I've never known Gus to apologise for anything much. He once said to me...well, he literally said, 'I'm not apologisin' for anythin'.' Those were his exact words."

"Mmm," Mrs. Vasani, Daya by forename, acknowledged. "I know what I'd be worried about," she moved the conversation on. "What'll happen if you and Herman are offered bigger gigs, and more money? If he starts acting like that again...well, quite frankly, who needs it?"

"I know," Rash nodded. "Oh, I don't get it. I mean, Gus writes great songs, he really does. And sure, he likes a drink, but...not usually like *that*." He let out an exasperated sigh. "I don't know. Lin can be just as bad. I mean, 'I don't think any of us are in a band right now.' What're you supposed to say to that?"

"Well, look—and this is putting it bluntly—she's got her own problems, hasn't she?" Daya said next. As one whose quiet, conservative lifestyle did not match Lin's, she'd given her son this speech before. "She's bad-tempered, Rashesh. She was like it the day I met her. And I'm sorry, but when you've just been beaten up on a bus, you're in no position to—"

Rash was already shaking his head. "Mum... *stop*. Lin wasn't beaten up. She was attacked by three idiots who were drunk, didn't like her appearance, and have no idea how to treat a woman. It wasn't her fault." He purposely sidestepped the subject of Lin's sexuality; his mother did not always boast the best understanding of the topic. "You are right about her being...fiery, though. She overreacts too often."

"Yes, she does," his mother affirmed. "And *you* don't deserve it. It wouldn't hurt her, or Gus, to show you and Herman a bit more respect."

"Well look," Mr. Vasani broke in at that point. "Why don't you give it a few days? You won't decide anything when everyone's tempers are flaring. I'd let it all simmer down first, and then talk." Gomtesh had stepped back, assessed the situation and made a rational suggestion; this was a strength that Rash admired in his father.

"Maybe you're right," he replied, still undecided.

"Well that's what I'd do," his father recommended. "Let 'em come to their senses. And if they don't, then you and Herman, or Fritz, or whatever his name is, can start your own band without the toxic twins in tow."

Gomtesh's playful use of language always brought a smile to Rash's face. If level-headedness was one thing his old man had tried to teach him, how to have a sense of humour was another. "They're cousins, dad," he reminded him. "But no, I get what you're saying."

- GUS, PT. I -

They must think I'm a loser. I bet they were all looking forward to today. And yesterday. I won't be able to hear the word "Sydney" again without feeling guilty. Or walk past The Smoke. If they let me back in!

They probably just think I'm thick. Ailish, Gracie, Danny and that boyfriend of his, Caleb. Sam, Auntie Jean, Mark, all of 'em—yeah, they're gonna be sitting round talking about me. "He can't handle his drink". "He's SO immature". Lin'll be rubbing it in. "Why are men such twats?" Well ha-ha-ha. I'm laughing, look!

What does she expect? An apology? Why's it always ME who's gotta apologise? There's no point in saying sorry anyway. Won't change anything. Oh...what's the fucking point in any of it? Why do I even bother? It's all well and good Josh and his wannabe Marxists sitting round, talking about climate change this, Sea Shepherd that, "direct action", blah blah blah. Look where "direct action" got me! I might as well have stayed home. ...Tell you what, I might as well just drink myself to death in a gutter somewhere. I'd be doing everyone a favour. If I ain't here, I can't disappoint anyone, can I?

Maybe I could take that douchebag down with me. Yeah, we'll have a duel. Guthrie Ward vs. I-Want-Wonderwall- 'Cause-It's-The-Only-Oasis-Song-EVER-And-If- I-Don't-Get-It-I'll-Ruin-Your-Gig! You're a dickhead, pal! Ever heard of "Don't Look Back In Anger"? "Songbird"? How about "Champagne Supernova"? Even in the van he wouldn't shut up. Well thanks for ruining my gig, douchebag. He needs taking out in the back yard and shooting. He's no use to mankind anyway.

...Jeez, is my stomach ever gonna get better? Since when did five pints do this? Alright, and a couple shots. But seriously, someone up there's against me. How'm I supposed to eat anything if I feel sick? ...I oughta just quit the booze. Straight up. Just go sober. It can't be much worse than this, can it? So much for all that writing the other

night. The hell was that all worth? "Alcohol brings out the best in me." Yeah, sure.

...Oh, SHUT UP. Get OUT of my head! Fucking "Lady In Black", I'm SICK of it. It's been going round and round in my head all day. This is what I mean—what is music, a blessing or a curse? Therapy or torture? What the hell was I given it for? Sometimes I wish I could just turn it off. Like a tap. Turn and DONE. It drives me mad.

...So what you gonna do, Gus? "I don't know, what d'you wanna do?" replied the vulture...no, STOP. I'm not going there again, either. Sorry Mr. Kipling, no time for ya. ...So what AM I gonna do?

...I don't know.

I really don't know.

- LIN, PT. I -

She had made the effort to message Logan, Kim and Jess, three friends from New Glasgow who'd promised to make the now-needless trip east. With that, everybody she could think of had been notified. Herman, meanwhile, had uploaded an official statement on behalf of the band, edited for about the thirtieth time. *We thank you for your understanding and would like to ask for privacy*, the final line had read. The world now knew about last night's fracas, and that St. Patrick's Day in Sydney was well and truly off the cards.

Currently, Lin was at the kitchen table with Mark, who had half an hour for her before his fishing match. Thoughtfully, he'd invited Lin along, but she had declined. "I wouldn't be very good company," she'd told him. She was, however, considering calling work, to see if Melanie could use an extra pair of hands in the afternoon. Surely it would be better than moping around the apartment on her own, with mum also out volunteering with the Mental Health Foundation in Dartmouth.

"So...has Gus done anythin' like this before?" Mark was asking now. He was trying to piece the story together for himself. *To connect the dots*, as Sam liked to say.

"Not really, no," Lin muttered. She took a sip of her water; she hadn't been in the mood for anything caffeinated. "I mean, I've seen him wasted at loads of gigs. But he's never *attacked* people." She shook her head resentfully. "He's takin' the advice of Josh and Mills. 'Righteous rage' my ass. They've got about as much sense as...well, I don't know what."

"What I don't understand is, why didn't he let the security guy deal with it?" Mark wondered. "He was about to, I saw him! Gus didn't need to get involved."

"I know!" Lin nodded. "He told me—Gus, I mean—he said he was 'trying to stand up for the band'. Well is that s'posed to make me feel better? 'Cause it *don't*."

Her voice took on a higher pitch as she became emotional.

"And *then*, he goes and blames *me*, actin' like it's *my* fault! '*Oh, why're you gettin' molested by three men on a bus?*' Bastard. I could have smacked him for that!"

"Yeah, there's no need for that," Mark agreed.

"I mean, I've tried my *fucking* best for him!" she despaired. "For the whole band! We're tryin' to be positive, waitin' *so* patiently for bigger gigs, more recognition, more fans, more money." Giving Mark a start, she slammed her fist down on the table. "What's the POINT in any of it?! It's all goin' to shit."

By now she was in tears. Mark rose calmly, walked around the table, and drew his stepdaughter to his sturdy figure. Lin, sobbing, hugged him back.

"It's hopeless!" she sniffed wretchedly. "I just want this band to do well, that's all! But we'll *never* catch a break, no matter what we do. It's like Skylight all over again!"

After a few seconds, Mark attempted to encourage her. "Look, don't give up," he said. "*You* did really well last night. The way you got everyone quiet like that, and playin' that song all on your own? That was *brilliant.*"

Lin got a hold of herself slightly. "You really think so?" she asked, misty-eyed.

"I don't think. I *know,*" he assured her with a confident nod. He released himself from Lin slightly, but still had a supportive hand to her shoulder. "Now obviously, I don't know much about music. But after last night...I respect what you do."

At that, Lin managed a wan smile. "Thanks Mark. That means a lot to me." She wiped away the tears, and exhaled long. "Look, I'm really sorry about all this."

"Don't be silly. I'll get you some tissues," he offered. He went into the living room. Unable to find what he was looking for, he told Lin he would check the bedroom.

She sat alone, a mess of emotions and a jumble of thoughts. Presently, Mark reappeared and handed her a pack of Kleenexes.

"I regret sayin' that, you know," she said as she dried her face.

"Saying what?" Mark asked.

"Tellin' Gus to get out of my life," Lin explained. "He's family, y'know? It's just that, after what happened with my dad, I've been afraid to trust m... many people. I mean, I *wanna* trust Gus, but how can I, when he does things like this?"

Mark offered a sympathetic nod. Lin looked down at the table, shaking her head and still sniffing back mucus.

"Well look...I need to load the car up in a minute," he reminded her. "What're you gonna do?"

"Christ knows," Lin sighed. She thought for a moment, and gave a more constructive reply. "I guess I might as well go into work. If Mel needs me. Sittin' in here'll only make it worse." On that note, she picked up her phone to make the call.

"All right then. I'll be downstairs if you need me. Okay?"

"All right. Thanks."

Mark turned and walked away. As he reached the door, Lin called after him.

"Mark?"

He turned back.

"Two things." She hesitated, then went for it. "Sorry about the fireworks. You know..." She motioned with her fist to the table top.

Mark laughed lightly. "Oh, don't worry about that. I've seen worse."

"No, seriously," she opened up. "Were they right? *Am* I too aggressive?"

He planned his answer, and opted for some honesty. "Yes, sometimes. Look, that's a different conversation. What was the other thing?"

"Thanks." She managed another faint smile. "For, you know, being there."

"Sure," he returned the sentiment. Then he went to pack for his fishing trip.

- HERMAN -

"You haven't had one of those in a while," was Ailish's comment.

"I know," Herman said, a little hoarse in the throat from his sneezing fit. "Maybe I *am* allergic to house dust."

"Mmm. You might wanna get it checked out," came the recommendation from Evan, Ailish's father. Being health-conscious was one by-product of having a wife with chronic fatigue.

The three of them sat at one of the small tables in The Hemlock, the Macdonald family restaurant. Sheena, Mrs. Macdonald, was at home, still battling the condition that would bite hard for periods and then let up for a while. The time was 4.25pm, meaning Herman would need to leave shortly so father and daughter could set everything up for dinner. Gracie and Nestor had also stopped by earlier in the afternoon, on their way back up to Lower Sackville. Nestor had been under the impression that the decision to cancel Sydney had been the band's. Herman and Ailish had enlightened him as to the real reason.

"Right, so hold on," he'd asked. "How did Sydney know what happened last night? It's not like they were there."

"I don't know," Herman had grimaced. "No-one knows! We think someone at The Smoke warned 'em. Like, maybe it was Martin, or the owners. Could've been someone in the audience, possibly. But don't ask me who, I've got no idea."

"Hmm," Nestor had mused. "Okay, sorry. I must've missed that part."

The five-way conversation over coffee had helped, but Herman still felt—as he'd put it to his wife-to-be several times—very sad. Currently he didn't know what was worse; the fact that Paddy's Day was ruined, or that the whole band might be over.

"You gonna be all right then, Ben?" Evan asked now. Naturally, Ailish's father never called him Herman, unless in the presence of others who only knew him as such.

"Yeah, I'll manage," he replied. He did not wholeheartedly believe it. "I'll find things to keep myself busy."

"If it's quiet later on, I'll come home early," Ailish reminded him.

"It's fine, sweetie," Herman repeated, sliding his hand across the table and taking hers. "You do what you gotta do." He opted for a slight change in subject. "To be honest, I'd be more worried about Gus."

"Yeah. You know, he's never struck me as the depressed type," Evan said. "I mean, it *is* hard growing up without a father. But whether that's relevant to any of this, I don't know. If it is, he certainly won't find the answers at the bottom of a bottle."

"I've never known him as depressed either," Herman affirmed. "But seriously, you guys shoulda seen him this morning. He was like frickin' Percy Wetmore. You know, the dude from *The Green Mile* who winds up all catatonic?"

"Mm-hmm," Ailish was already nodding. "And Tam isn't really herself right now, either. Even that song she did last night—it was electrifying, but it's like she was *possessed*, or exorcising a demon or something. I've never seen anything like it."

"Exactly," Herman murmured. He shrugged his shoulders, then got to his feet. "Anyway, I should go. Don't wanna hold you guys up."

"Okay honey. Can I get a kiss first?"

"*Na klar*," Herman replied, with a smile. He'd taught Ailish that much German. She rose from her chair and he duly obliged.

"See you tonight," he finished. Then he turned to Evan. "Do you want a kiss too?"

"Err...no, I'll pass," Mr. Macdonald smirked. He extended his hand as usual.

"Have a good evening," Herman grinned. "Hope it all goes well." He put his jacket (navy blue) on, said a final bye, and went out into the late afternoon.

Herman's lightning blue Ford Escape was one of the few vehicles in the near-empty parking lot. By 7pm tonight, it would be almost full, with scores of Paddy's Day revellers stopping by on their way into Downtown. *Damn*, Herman thought again at that moment. *Paddy's Day. That should have been us.*

He unlocked the car and got in. Before starting the engine, he sat and contemplated what might have been. Knowing he was missing tonight's festivities, and yet not feeling like celebrating them one bit, was a bitter pill to swallow. A weight heavy upon his heart and a gnawing in his stomach. Eventually, he shook his head and took out his phone, to check for any last-minute messages before setting off.

There was only one notification there. It was a text from Manfred, a South African pal of his who kept in touch more regularly than most, though usually it was to send him funny videos that had gone viral online. Tempted to leave it till later, Herman decided to read the message.

Sure enough, it contained a video link, with a brief message above it. *Dude! Have you seen this?*

"*Na gut Mani, dann zeig mal,*" Herman sighed to himself. *Go on then Mani, let's see it.* He tapped on the link.

And as the video played and Herman recognised, with mounting incredulity, what he was watching—and the number of *views* it had—he couldn't believe his eyes.

- GUS, PT. II -

Footsteps and the pitter-patter of paws approached the slightly ajar bedroom door. Alison pushed it open and, ever the faithful friend, Archie came trotting in with her. Gus, now wearing a fresh shirt, made the effort to swing himself into a sitting position on the bed. He reached out with his left hand and ruffled the dog's dense, wavy coat.

Alison, Mrs. Ward, had put on her Emilies, purple raincoat and grey pashmina scarf in preparation for taking the dog out. Going for walkies had proven challenging for the energetic Berner when they'd first got him five years ago. With some home training, and a little patience from his new owners, he'd grown to accept the collar and leash.

"It's not raining out there," she reported, making three paces towards the window. "Just a bit cloudy. You sure you don't wanna come?"

Still uncannily quiet, Gus shook his head lightly. He looked off to the side.

"You know where I take him, I'll only be an hour," she said. Gus offered a slight nod. "Well, unless Sue Paige is over there. That damn woman never stops talking."

He continued to look away as his mum beckoned Archie over. On their way out into the hall, she turned and stood for a moment. Contemplating her son.

Gus, who hadn't said a word all afternoon, finally opened his mouth.

"What's it like havin' an alkie as a son?"

Initially, Alison said nothing. After five seconds' silence, she answered. "Guthrie, you're not an *alkie*."

Gus, with further effort, cast his eyes up to hers. "Criminal, then."

At that, she came back in. Dutifully the dog followed. Bowing, she kissed her son on the head and gave his black hair a quick stroke.

"It's gonna be all right, boy," she promised. Her eyes burned into his. "Trust me, you'll all get through this together." She turned back towards the hall. "I should know, I'm world champion at gettin' through things."

Half a minute later, the front door clicked shut. He heard the keys turning in the lock, and then mum and Archie were gone.

Gus sat alone in the apartment, surrounded by the silence that had never felt so stark. Nor so cold.

All right, he thought then. *Here goes.*

With his right hand he reached into his pocket.

- LIN, PT. II -

Business at Café Payat was achingly slow. Aside from two female students, and a fiftysomething guy with greying dreadlocks and a copy of *StarMetro*, the place was dead. Mel was currently out back, looking for an invoice or a form or something; Lin had been too absorbed in her own thoughts to hear properly.

A minute ago, though it had felt like longer, she'd had another look at her phone. Still no messages from Rash or Herman. Or from Gus. *He can't have meant that*, she tried to assure herself again. *He knows I was attacked! Why would he say that?*

As she wiped the coffee bar down again (there was little else to do), she still felt miserable. The live version of Sheryl Crow's "C'mon C'mon" playing over the café speakers, with lyrics about mind games and heartbreak, was only making it worse. Yet again she tried to suppress the events of the past 24 hours. But she knew they would return soon enough. All it would take was a trigger, something to associate with it all.

So what're you gonna do? she asked herself, for the umpteenth time during her shift. And for the umpteenth time, the same answer. *I don't fucking know.*

What she did know—or at least had to accept—was that she needed to control her temper. The irascible attitude, the raised voice, the profanity, *definitely* the way she'd behaved towards Gus and Herman that morning. None of it had helped; more to the point, it was embarrassing, both to her and to her friends. *If I ain't careful*, she scolded herself, *I'll end up hitting someone. Christ, it'll be me going down for assault next.* She knew well that violence was wrong, as if the horrors of Wednesday night hadn't been a reminder! But what could she do to address her aggression issues? She had no idea where to start, and her only inkling was defeatist. *Maybe I can't change.* If Mel's reappearance didn't help solve the conundrum, it was at least a distraction.

"Did you find it?" Lin asked.

"Yep," she inhaled, paperwork in hand. "One less thing to worry about."

Lin offered half a nod, looking on across the shop floor. Making herself a coconut latte, the shift manager saw that her assistant still wasn't feeling her best.

"Go on hon, you take off," she offered. "Go to your mum's. Some mother-daughter time'll be just what the doctor ordered."

"You sure?"

"Yeah, don't worry about me. It's hardly busy."

"True. Yeah, mum should be home by the time I get back."

"You remember what I said, okay?" Mel reminded her.

"'Friends and family are the best therapy'," Lin repeated. That drove the knife in again, as Gus and the others *were* friends and family. Fortunately, not the only ones.

"That's the one," she smiled with a thumbs-up. "See you tomorrow at...ten-thirty, eh?"

"All right. Thanks, Mel."

Having ditched her apron for her leather jacket, Lin stepped out into the grey afternoon. Immediately, she pulled out her vape pen and took a much-needed drag. She tilted her head back, exhaling a stream of smooth mint and bitter discontent. The thought of not going to Cape Breton with her band, the mental picture of anywhere up to 30,000 people celebrating St. Patrick's Day without them—it hurt. The pain was real; at times it was sickening.

Her Honda was parked a five-minute walk away on Mumford Road. On the way she vaped some more, only to chastise herself for breaking her promise of Wednesday night. *I said I'd quit. The hell was that worth?* Twice more she took out her phone as she went. Nothing.

Stop it, Tamila, she rebuked herself. *You'll drive yourself mad.* She tried to focus on what was around her—the buildings, the trees and the cars. But keeping her mind from wandering was impossible.

She reached the car and got in. Before moving off, temptation once more got the better of her. Another look at her phone. Nothing.

See? she thought, slinging it onto the passenger seat. *No further forward, am I?* Feeling as bad as when she'd set off from home, she reached up to start the engine.

Her phone rang.

Steadying herself for a second, just to be sure she wasn't imagining it, she looked over at the display. Yes, it was ringing. It was Herman.

Okay, she steeled herself. Nervously, she picked up the phone and answered.

"Hello."

"Lin! You gotta listen to me!" said her excited bandmate on the other end. "There's a video of last night with your song in it! It's going viral on social media!"

Lin, to begin with, was simply confused. "Sorry, what?"

Herman repeated himself, almost word for word.

Not sure if she was being screwed with or not, Lin sought clarification. "Right, hold on. What are you talking about? *What* video?"

"Oh—sorry! Someone...someone made a video of what happened in the pub," Herman composed himself. "Someone in the audience. They filmed the entire thing!"

"Eh?" Lin gasped. "Are you serious?!"

"Yeah!" Herman insisted. "I wouldn't lie about something like this!" He calmed himself again. "It's some guy called Ricky On The Road. That's his handle. He's a travel blogger or something. He got it all, Lin—the drunk guy spillin' his drink, Gus jumpin' off stage, the fight, both of 'em gettin' pulled away. And then your song!"

"What, all of it?!"

"Yeah! Right till the end, when the clapping stopped. The guy's edited it and put it up, he's called it 'Stay Safe This St. Patrick's Day', or something. Now people are sharing it, a lot!"

Lin was shocked. "Christ! I had no idea *anyone* filmed any of it!"

"Neither did I!" Herman echoed. "All I could think about was Ailish—you know, keepin' her safe."

"So...hold on a sec," Lin asked. She was struggling to think clearly. "What did you say about it goin' viral?" She was almost afraid to ask. "I mean...how many views?"

"Forty thousand and counting."

"Oh my God, WHAT?!" Lin spluttered, jolting forward in the driver's seat. "Herman, you're bullshitting me!"

"I'm not, I swear! I'll send ya the link! You see for yourself."

Lin was virtually speechless. "I...I can't believe it! Does The Smoke kn–"

"Wait—there's more," Herman interrupted, not letting up. "The guy mentioned *us*. He wrote 'Kilmainen' in the video description, he's linked to our channel, too! We're gettin' shares, subscribes, *comments*, Lin! Not only about the fight, but about your song. One woman's already askin' us when we're gonna record it in the studio."

"That...that's in*sane*!" Lin managed to stutter. Two minutes ago, she'd been a despondent part-time waitress; now suddenly she was some form of mini-celebrity on social media. She didn't know whether to be thrilled because of the song, scared for the violence beforehand, or both.

"And the streaming, too," Herman was continuing. "That's going up as well. It's *mad*, Lin! And it wasn't even 24 hours yet!"

"I...I don't know what to say!" she choked. With all that Herman had told her, whether or not The Smoke knew about this—and how they might react—seemed strangely trivial. Before she could speak further, Herman practically answered her next question for her.

"*That* must be how Sydney found out," he deduced. "They must've seen the video online! I don't think anyone at The Smoke called 'em at all."

"Right—so, hold on," Lin again tried to steady the ship. "Do Gus and Rash know about any o' this?"

"Well...no I don't think so!" Herman said, still speaking faster than usual. "I've only just found out myself. But listen, Lin! We can't give up now. This is *real*. People are taking notice of us!"

At that moment, Lin knew exactly what they needed to do. Just as she'd known the night before.

"Come on," Herman was persuading her. "We can get over all this, I know we can! Let's talk to Gus, sort all this crap out, and make it work!"

Lin, who needed no persuasion, couldn't wait to get her answer out. "Herman, hang up! Call Rash!" she instructed him hurriedly. "And send me the video. I'll call Gus!"

Herman quickly agreed, and ended the call. Lin punched in her PIN and went to bring up her phonebook. But before she could get that far, a message arrived for her.

It was from Gus.

She hesitated for a second, then tapped on it.

And as she read what her cousin had written, new tears began to break in her eyes.

They were tears of relief. Tears of *joy*.

CAIBIDEIL A DEICH
CHAPTER TEN

The Reward

EPILOGUE

Behind a curtain of concrete they stand. Waiting. *Hiding.* Mist is upon their breath, the ice of late winter and the raging fires of anticipation, burning brighter than ever. They can hear what awaits on the other side, they feel the tide lifting their hearts on its flow and ebb. They were born for moments like these. The city outside bathes silent in the cool light of silver; in here, it will be hot under explosive rays of red, yellow and more.

As the man before them says two minutes, the events of eleven months ago are a world away. That was over there and this is over here. They have all felt much better—stronger—and fortune has smiled kindly upon them. The chatter around them has matured into healthy interest, earning them and their music acclaim from further online influencers. Invitations and collaborations in pastures old and new have followed, while persistent promotion and engagement have widened the net further. The algorithms, too, began to take notice as the statistics entered four-, five- and then six-figure territory. And even the profits crept up as the realisation took hold that it *is* all possible. That a life *cannot* be condemned to second or third best, not without fight. And now here they are, riding on the back of giants in Canada's eighth city for the opening night of their first nationwide tour. A tour with fourteen stops and some glowing prospects.

They have all grown, and not apart. The anger of Lin has made way for serenity, for the calmer waters of meditation. Resentment now cedes the passage to apology, and forgiveness does follow. And yes, the moods once marred by intoxication are—for the present, at least—nurtured by new tastes, by pursuits and pleasures less destructive. The scenes of their March 16th had resulted in a fine to pay, nothing more, while their aggressors of that week had not fared so well. Such experiences build strength; the spark, the fire, the *edge* can only gain in potency. When an individual falters, he or she is caught by those walking alongside. They are samaritan hands on a stony path. Persistence is their father, their mother is hope. And she, let us not forget, is one who springs eternal.

The quartet's giant, beating heart skips as the walk-on music chimes into view. The quiet before the storm, tinkering melodies and sighing chords. The music of the soul. Gus has an air of maturity about him these days, as he warms his voice with a note or four. Lin, now smoke-free since August, smiles and gives her cousin an affectionate hug. They thank one another—and their bandmates—for the reciprocal friendship and support. For how, even in their darkest hours, at least one of them will find the resolve to continue. For how, even given the lucky breaks, it is ultimately their *resilience* that has taken them this far.

This is it. This is what they've always wanted. They've been tried by fire—now this is the reward. To stand on the very precipice of the world. As the audience begins to clap in time to the music, they wonder just how many are out there tonight. They find out as they take the dark passage to the stage, and emerge with hands and hearts aloft to meet the lion roar that fills the room.

What a joy it is, to see how many have come! Blue light cascades, sweeping in and out of amber fireflies, droplets of dew above a sea of faces. Behind the large, empty Oloroso sherry cask, the musicians take their places. From left to right they stand a heroic percussionist, a genius songsmith, a newly wed eight-stringer, and an ever-dependable accordionist.

And at the very summit of anticipation the background music drops, leaving silence in its wake.

And then they start to play.

They are Kilmainen. A Celtic folk-punk band. And if you're in here tonight, they're absolutely everything.

Andy Beck

Kilmainen are:

Guthrie "Gus" Ward – lead vocals, acoustic guitar
Tamila "Lin" Ward – bodhrán, percussion, backing vocals
Benjamin "Herman" Macdonald – mandolin, tin whistle, backing vocals
Rashesh "Rash" Vasani – accordion, keys, backing vocals

"Kilmainen" is an intentional misspelling of *Kilmainham* (Irish: *Cill Mhaighneann*), the jail where fourteen Irish republican leaders were executed after the Easter Rising of 1916. The executions angered the public, and fuelled support for the independence of Ireland from the United Kingdom.

YOU'VE READ THE BOOK.
ARE YOU READY TO FOLLOW YOUR OWN DREAMS?

THIS IS MY NAME
niche. accountability. marketing. earnings.

FIND YOUR NICHE.
CONNECT WITH THE RIGHT PEOPLE.
MASTER ONLINE MARKETING.
GET PAID TO DO WHAT YOU LOVE!

Access your free video training on
AndyBeckWriting.com

Read on for more information.

ACTION PLAN

How to Follow Your Own Dreams

First of all, thank you for reading my story. I hope it has taken you on an emotionally charged, musical ride of peaks and troughs! If so, and if you can relate to the struggle for success endured (but ultimately won) by the four musicians, then I have good news for you. You, too, can follow your dreams. You can do something—not necessarily music—that you are genuinely passionate about, and get paid to do it. Whether it's a full-time income or just a side salary that you would like to earn from it, you will still be making a difference, both to your own life and to the lives of those who pay for your work.

You may be wondering why your happiness and personal success would matter to me. The simple answer is, I have struggled to achieve both in my life.

We are encouraged by the world around us to work long hours for somebody else, sometimes 50–60 hours a week, just for financial reward and social status. I'm sure that many of your family members and friends do this. But there's a problem; depending on which studies you read, anywhere between 45% and a staggering 80% of the employed are unhappy with their work[1]. Their negative attitudes can range from boredom and disenchantment, to a deep hatred and resentment of their job and colleagues. This is unsettling, given how many weeks of work remain ahead of us in the one life we get to enjoy.

In this regard, I opted for a different path a few years ago. I currently work a job with reduced hours that covers the bills, whilst freeing up the time I need for my writing and musical output. I love my creative pursuits too much to let them dwindle as mere hobbies, and some of my personal heroes—American entrepreneur Scott Dinsmore and Swiss composer Adrian von Ziegler, to name but two different examples—have walked some inspiring, life-affirming paths that I, too, wish to walk. You can follow in the steps of your own idols, too, if the prospect sounds appealing to you (you're reading this book, so I'm guessing it does).

Of course, such paths are not conventional. They certainly don't match the advice a careers advisor or recruitment agency would give you. But despite what you may have been led to believe, you <u>can</u> enjoy a life on your own terms, or at least, *more* on your own terms. You can identify what it is that you love, do that very thing, and get paid for it in both financial and spiritual terms. Perhaps you can now appreciate that my lifelong love of music was not my only motivation for writing *Folk Springs Eternal*.

Nevertheless, I will strike a note of caution. As the story of Gus, Lin, Herman and Rash develops, it becomes clear that the quartet's dreams of "making it" as musicians will be met with scorn, hostility and, in some cases, even outbreaks of violence. Chapters 3 and 4 are the first signs of this, when Herman has to deal with some rather unflattering tripe on social media, and Rash's office colleagues disregard his nonconformist thinking. If that all seems rather harmless, look at how quickly things degenerate thereafter:

Chapter 5	Lin's attack on the bus
Chapter 7	Gus's arrest (admittedly for drunken fighting)
Chapter 8	Cancellation of band's Cape Breton show
	Gus and Lin's acrimonious falling out
	The end of the band?
Chapter 9	Rash advised to cease working with Gus and Lin
	Gus depressed, possibly contemplating suicide
	Herman and Lin despairing

While your own path may not hold all of the above in store, an uphill struggle does stand between you and the success you desire. But it is a fight worth waging; the about-turn from sorrow to jubilation at the end of Chapter 9, followed by the exciting future depicted in the Epilogue, are precisely what the band deserves for passing its "trial by fire". It is the musicians' payoff for the experiences (and in some cases, the *learning*) that they have each gone through. A catharsis reflected perfectly in Lin's tears.

So yes, it's a tough path to walk. Phases of your own journey will require a considerable push beyond your comfort zone; furthermore, you are always likely to encounter resistance when you take your own dreams more seriously. When I walked away from my old, "safe" 40-hour job in software auditing, to find my current reduced hours and concentrate more on my writing and music, my family were horrified. It's an unpleasant storm to navigate, when those closest to you say that you're making a huge mistake, throwing your career away, committing financial suicide, etc. And besides, it takes time, sometimes *years*, to wean yourself off the day job (either partially or completely) and turn your side venture into a profitable business.

BUT: is it impossible? No. And for any difficulty you may encounter, you will also find support among those who *do* understand. These people might be old friends, new friends you'll make along the way, or a small handful of family members. Interestingly, nearly all of my colleagues in my old job congratulated me on my decision to reduce my office hours. Perhaps they knew I was aiming for something a little higher than the hand that many of us believe we've been dealt.

So again, is it impossible to follow your dreams? To live a life more aligned with your true principles and passions? Again, no it isn't. You have what it takes to change the course of your life, no matter what your age or experiences. You can grow in confidence and knowledge, as I have done over the past three years, and slowly begin to enjoy the success that your efforts deserve.

Below, I give you five tips to get started. The following advice forms part of your **THIS IS MY NAME** video training, which can be accessed for free on my website at andybeckwriting.com. My intention is to provide realistic, practical advice supported by some real-life examples, and broadly following the formula set forth by Scott Dinsmore. In his TED talk that has over 5 million views (and counting), the late entrepreneur outlines his simple three-step recipe:

Become a self-expert.
Do the impossible.
Surround yourself with passionate people[2].

Do any of these steps represent new territory to you? Fear not! All three are within your capabilities, as you will discover.

TIP #1
Do what honestly makes you happy.

Hobbies, or the activities we derive enjoyment from, are crucial in that they tell us something about ourselves. They reflect our inner nature, the principles we believe in and the kinds of people we like to spend time with. Given that hobbies make life much more pleasurable (indeed, worth living), can you imagine how exciting it would be to indulge those passions on a more professional level? To live by your morals and work with some inspirational, like-minded people in the form of your own business?

Before I go any further, you may have noticed that I've used the word *business* more than once now. This is deliberate choice, even if the word may be uncomfortable to some. My advice applies not only to writers and musicians like myself, but to anyone working in any domain within the entertainment industry or outside of it. You certainly don't have to play an instrument, write a story, paint pottery or sketch landscapes to do something that makes you happy! Since I started co-hosting personal development meetups in London in 2016, I have spoken to lawyers, therapists, university lecturers, performance coaches, charity workers, fashion designers and individuals from various other fields of activity. The two traits that I always recognise in these people are a.) a burning passion, and b.) a desire to do something with it. To give something to the world and make it that little bit happier and more harmonious.

As such, no matter who you are or what you're interested in, don't be put off by the term *business*. I speak from experience when I assure you that enjoying financial success does not compromise the integrity of your work—not unless you allow it to. By offering your ideas to the world, you are improving the quality of life for those who like your kind of output. You are fulfilling a need of theirs, and do you deserve to be paid for that? Yes, of course! Even Gus, one of the less commercially minded members of Kilmainen, knows this in chapter one. "I ain't a moneyhead, but that's what musicians SHOULD get paid." That line captures it well; I don't recommend that you prioritise earnings over integrity, but I do believe that you should earn enough to make an income that you are satisfied with. Gus again weighs this up well in Chapter 6, when he pours his thoughts and philosophies into his journal.

So how do you do, or even *know*, what makes you happy? Some individuals are fortunate, in that they can point to one specific passion that they have. For my cousin-in-law, it's dancing, and she runs her own studio and various projects. For my best friend's brother, it's football (soccer, if you're in North America), and he was semi-professional for a time. Now ask yourself: did you do something recently that absorbed you so completely, something that you so thoroughly enjoyed, that you lost track of time? If so, *that* could be your calling. Something where you make not only yourself happy, but surely others, too.

Some people, of course, have more than one talent. And this is normal. I am certainly no exception, given my strong interest in both writing and music. Separate interests may be combinable, or you might have to pursue them individually; that will depend on the hobbies in question and how you perceive their marketability. However, begin by just figuring out what passions and values drive you, and whether you would like to take them more seriously. It doesn't even matter if your area of interest doesn't appear to be an established trend (more on this under Tip #5). Passion cannot be measured by widespread popularity alone; we can't all be pop stars, or there'd be no underground artists! If something feels real to you, then it is. And it'll be worth pursuing, because believe me, there are others out there who are just as keen on that hobby as you are.

Tip #2
Think of ways to make income and an impact.

This is the next obvious step. Once you've identified your strongest interest(s), start thinking of ways to monetise it, or them. As demonstrated in *Folk Springs Eternal*, it is possible to create more than one stream of income from your passion; for Kilmainen, there is music streaming, CD sales, merchandise sales, and royalties from performances or broadcasting. Other ideas might have included giving music lessons, guest-featuring on other bands' songs and helping to record other musicians' work. In terms of making a positive impact on others, the last three of these suggestions are especially relevant.

When planning the monetisation of your work, no idea is ridiculous, and no target is too small. Begin by noting some ideas that you would

a.) enjoy making or producing;
b.) be able to make or produce quite quickly;
c.) be able to sell.

An example may look like the one below.

Passion:

• Mental health awareness

Ideas:

- Host charity events with a small financial target;

- Run paid workshops based around e.g. meditation, CBT or hypnotherapy;

- Write, self-publish and promote a book on the subject;

- Start a blog, vlog, social media channel, etc. to promote your work and your cause.

Criteria to fulfil:

a.) Would I enjoy doing the above? -> <u>yes</u>/no
b.) Could I organise all of the above quite quickly? -> <u>yes</u>/no
c.) Could I make an income, and an impact, by doing it? -> <u>yes</u>/no

Mental health awareness is just one example, albeit a highly important one in today's world. And of course, what is meant by "quite quickly" under criterion b.) will differ from passion to passion, and thus is open to interpretation. How quickly will people expect to see a finished product from you? What will that product be? How many such products will you need in order for people to take you seriously? And how much time can you set aside for the preparations?

Finding the time required for your work is explored in the next tip. In THIS IS MY NAME, I also explore the importance of asking others for help, which some individuals (including myself, a year or two ago!) can be too afraid or proud to do. For now, who can you think of in your chosen field(s) who is making money and a good impression on their followers and clients? What pointers can they give you on how to get started? Write down the names of individuals or small businesses that come to mind, and then make the effort to contact them. You have nothing to lose! Many people are happy to share with you how they got started, made their first earnings, and have kept their clients coming back ever since.

Tip #3
Spend 25 minutes a day on it.

One factor often cited by people as a reason, or perhaps an *excuse*, for not doing something is the all-important factor of time. "I've been *so* busy lately", "I haven't got round to it", "I haven't got time", etc. Do any of these phrases sound familiar? What may surprise you is that you don't actually *need* a lot of time, at least not in the early stages of an idea. When a project is first conceived, its creator often pictures a mountain of labour, hours invested, pitfalls, and learning en route to eventual success. Standing at the foot of said mountain, gawping upwards, you may feel very small—indeed, overwhelmed.

Never fear! Turning a passion into a paid venture can be done in short, regular bursts. You will make far quicker progress by doing just 25 minutes' work a day than by one long session per week. This is due to the regularity with which you apply yourself; frequent input means less time to forget where you were, and what you've achieved so far. An analogy, while not strictly involving 25 minutes a day (nor a business), is my own story of learning to drive. While many learners opt for one lesson a week, I had the idea of taking two a week. This got me behind the wheel once every three or four days, a regularity that was much more conducive to remembering everything and making smooth progress. I certainly didn't start life as a gifted driver, but I got my licence within five months. Some people I know, who took just one lesson a week, needed a year or more to pass.

The 25-minutes-a-day approach is feasible, since almost anyone can apply it to their own schedule. Unless you have a pretty cast-iron excuse, you're not going to tell me you can't find 25 minutes a day to work on your business! If the idea of working on it every day is still unrealistic, then opt for 4–6 days a week. I promise that the progress you'll make will surprise you, and others. By way of contrast, believing that long sessions are required for the job can lead to inconsistent progress, difficulty getting back on track, complacency and other negative, unhelpful complications. Put my advice to the test instead; plus, once you become engrossed in the task at hand, you may well find yourself working at it for longer than 25 minutes, which can only be of further benefit.

Working in short bursts can, admittedly, feel painstakingly slow, like chipping away at a rock until the sculpture is finally complete. However, a more positive analogy can be found in the popular James N. Watkins quote. "A river cuts through rock, not because of its power, but because of its persistence." You will find that this is true for you, too; with endurance and a sensible strategy, something will eventually give. It is true that Kilmainen are fortunate when Ricky On The Road's video of their St. Patrick's gig starts to go viral. However, to put the band's subsequent successes down to luck would be missing the point. Success is *not* primarily dependent on good fortune, even if lucky breaks are helpful. It is self-belief, perseverance, and calculated decisions that will guide you to your goals, be they financial or otherwise.

Tip #4
Someone out there is already doing it.

Some entrepreneurs mistakenly believe that nobody else is interested in their hobby, less still in their attempts to popularise it. If this is you, then think again. As Scott Dinsmore declared in his TED talk, "I don't care what it is that you're into. If you're into knitting, you can find someone who is killing it at knitting"[3]. The man had a point; your ambitious objective to convert passion into pay suddenly seems more realistic when you consider others who have already succeeded at it. Very rarely will you walk a path in this life that hasn't already been navigated—successfully—by somebody else among the billions of people out there. Sometimes, you just need to find such a person to draw inspiration from.

That being said, please don't fall into the trap of thinking, "oh, that's already been done, so nobody will be interested in my take on it." The opposite is true; the fact that others are already excelling in your field should be of reassurance to you. Healthy competition is a natural part of the game, and as such is not to be feared. Indeed, folk music, the subject of my story, is very much alive given that bands and solo artists continue to spring up all over the globe. Even if The Pogues are the godfathers of Celtic punk music, the scene didn't stop with them in the 1980s (otherwise the term "godfathers" would be redundant). The impeccable Julie Fowlis may have established herself as a leading Scottish Gaelic singer in the 2000s, but that hasn't prevented others from trying their hand at the genre. Let us consider a corporate example, too; at the time of writing, Bose and Sony are the giants of high-end noise-cancelling headphones. But that's not to say that other competitors can't have a go— especially when each player brings different designs, gimmicks and, of course, prices to the table.

All in all, people appreciate variety. The next tip expands further upon this point.

Tip #5
It's okay to be niche!

Under Tip #1, I stated that a hobby does not have to be an established trend, as passion cannot be measured by popularity. This will be of especial relevance to you if you see yourself as having a *niche* interest. Far from cutting you off from a prospective audience, niches are actually beneficial, in that they help you to stand out from the masses. Especially in the age of online marketing, where so many people are vying for space and attention.

Even if you don't see your chosen field as being particularly niche, there is probably still a certain quirkiness, or "edge" to your approach. Do you offer something unique, something that very few others offer? If so, this could be your chance to stand out. *Niching down* to something that will earn you a core of loyal customers is a good basis upon which to build a business and income.

Let us take Leah McHenry as an example. A Canadian singer-songwriter, Leah's music has been described as "female-fronted Celtic symphonic metal". If your reaction to that is "female-fronted *what?*", then good! Believe it or not, this is a real micro-genre of music that blends heavy metal, female vocals, folk music (primarily the harp) and classical arrangements (e.g. string sections). While all four of these ingredients are effectively independent music styles in their own right, there are music lovers out there—myself included—who enjoy all of them, and thus are open to Leah's niche material. She has managed to build a following of adoring *superfans*, to use her term, and financially it is working extremely well for her. Leah generates over $100,000 a year[4] in earnings, all through knowing her market and targeting her prospective fans in a business-savvy manner—in the same way that a regular, more "mainstream" business would.

Leah's unorthodox but factual success story is a call to arms for any entrepreneur looking to shake the market up with something maverick. While an annual six-figure sum is not something I guarantee you, you can still achieve a degree of success that is satisfactory to you, by bringing your work to the attention of a small but highly dedicated client base. This is a much more sure-fire approach than making the common mistake of engaging in "hope marketing", i.e. sharing details of your work everywhere without any real knowledge of your target market, and praying that someone important or influential will take notice.

Your Next Step

Have the above tips got you fired up and ready to personalise your Action Plan? If so, **THIS IS MY NAME** is for you. The program consists of a free video training, followed by an online course, both of which will help you to start following your own dreams and enjoying the success that you deserve! Sign up in order to a.) identify your passion and "niche", b.) find people who will hold you accountable to your goals, c.) master online marketing (beginning with free traffic), and d.) generate earnings and impact by doing what you love.

THIS IS MY NAME
niche. accountability. marketing. earnings.

AndyBeckWriting.com

Endnotes

[1] According to Gallup polls, and studies conducted by Deloitte.
[2] See Scott's TED talk, *How to find and do work you love,* available on YouTube and other video platforms.
[3] Scott Dinsmore, *How to find and do work you love.*
[4] According to an article about Leah on unconventionallifeshow.com.

About the Author

ANDY BECK is a devoted writer, musician and multilinguist. He believes that each and every one of us has a story; a deep passion that can guide us on a journey of self-discovery and growth towards the life we really want. Andy inspires others to walk this path via his writing, music, social media content, public speaking and coaching.

In his twenties, Andy struggled to break the mental hold that the scripted, 9-to-5 lifestyle has over many of us. Now, Andy currently works a job with reduced hours, which pays the bills but frees up the time and energy required for his written and musical work. His writing conveys a positive, yet practical message to assist others in finding their own passion, getting the right people on their side, targeting their audience correctly, and getting paid to do it.

Andy and his amazing wife Kerstin split their time between Glasgow, Scotland and Maidstone, England.